CHANT OF DRUMS

Thrum, thrum, thrum, came the ceaseless sound of the drums: war and death (they said); blood and lust; human sacrifice and human feast! The soul of Africa, the spirit of the jungle, the gods men knew when dawns were young, beast-eyed, gaping-mouthed, huge-bellied, bloody-handed, the Black Gods (sang the drums). Kane stepped out of the thick jungle and came upon a plainly defined trail. Beyond, through the trees came the gleam of the village fires, flames glowing through the palisades. Kane walked down the trail swiftly.

He went silently and warily, sword extended in front of him . . . like a dark ghost he moved; alertly he stared; yet no warning came first to him, as a great, vague bulk rose up out of the shadows and struck him down . . .

ALAS, BABYLON by Pat Frank
BEASTS by John Crowley
A CANTICLE FOR LEIBOWITZ by
  Walter M. Miller, Jr.
CINNABAR by Edward Bryant
CRITICAL MASS by Frederik Pohl & C. M. Kornbluth
THE DAY OF THE DRONES by A. M. Lightner
THE DAY THE GODS DIED by Walter Ernsting
DEMON SEED by Dean Koontz
DHALGREN by Samuel R. Delany
DRAGONSONG by Anne McCaffrey
DRAGONSINGER by Anne McCaffrey
FANTASTIC VOYAGE by Isaac Asimov
THE FEMALE MAN by Johanna Russ
GLADIATOR-AT-LAW by Frederik Pohl &
  C. M. Kornbluth
THE GOLDEN SWORD by Janet E. Morris
HELLSTROM'S HIVE by Frank Herbert
THE HEPHAESTUS PLAGUE by Thomas Page
HIGH COUCH OF SILISTRA by Janet E. Morris
THE JONAH KIT by Ian Watson
KAMPUS by James E. Gunn
KULL by Robert E. Howard
LOGAN'S RUN by William F. Nolan &
  George Clayton Johnson
LOGAN'S WORLD by William F. Nolan
MAN PLUS by Frederik Pohl
A MAZE OF DEATH by Philip K. Dick
MONUMENT by Lloyd Biggle, Jr.
THE MYSTERIOUS ISLAND by Jules Verne
NOVA by Samuel R. Delany
NEBULA AWARD STORIES ELEVEN edited by
  Ursula K. Le Guin
THE POWER OF THE SERPENT by
  Peter Valentine Timlett
ROGUE IN SPACE by Fredric Brown
SEARCH THE SKY by Frederik Pohl &
  C. M. Kornbluth
SKULLS IN THE STARS by Robert E. Howard
THE 3 STIGMATA OF PALMER ELDRITCH by
  Philip K. Dick
THE TIME MACHINE by H. G. Wells
TRITON by Samuel R. Delany
TWILIGHT OF THE SERPENT by
  Peter Valentine Timlett
20,000 LEAGUES UNDER THE SEA by Jules Verne
UBIK by Philip K. Dick
WIND FROM THE ABYSS by Janet E. Morris
WHAT MAD UNIVERSE by Fredric Brown

#1
SOLOMON KANE

Skulls in the Stars

BY ROBERT E. HOWARD

Introduction by J. Ramsey Campbell

BANTAM BOOKS
TORONTO · NEW YORK · LONDON

RL 9, IL 8-up

SOLOMON KANE #1: SKULLS IN THE STARS
A Bantam Book / December 1978

Map by Tim Kirk

ACKNOWLEDGMENTS

Skulls in the Stars, copyright 1928 by Popular Fiction Publishing Company for Weird Tales, January 1929.

The Right Hand of Doom, copyright © 1968 by Glenn Lord for Red Shadows.

Red Shadows, copyright 1928 by Popular Fiction Publishing Company for Weird Tales, August 1928.

Rattle of Bones, copyright 1929 by Popular Fiction Publishing Company for Weird Tales, June 1929.

Part of The Castle of the Devil originally appeared in Red Shadows, copyright © 1968 by Glenn Lord. The complete version appears here for the first time.

The Moon of Skulls, copyright 1930 by Popular Fiction Publishing Company for Weird Tales, June, July 1930.

The One Black Stain, copyright © 1962 by Glenn Lord for The Howard Collector, Spring 1962.

Blades of the Brotherhood, copyright © 1968 by Glenn Lord for Red Shadows.

ISBN 0-553-12031-X

Published simultaneously in the United States and Canada

Bantam Books are published by Bantam Books, Inc. Its trademark, consisting of the words "Bantam Books" and the portrayal of a bantam, is registered in the United States Patent Office and in other countries. Marca Registrada. Bantam Books, Inc., 666 Fifth Avenue, New York, New York 10019.

PRINTED IN THE UNITED STATES OF AMERICA

CONTENTS

UPPER
BOGANDA
VILLAGE

AKAANA

SLAVERS' ROUTE

MAUSOLEUM

VILLAGE

CANNIBALS

CITY OF
NINN

LAKE
NYAYNA

OLD
BOGANDA

LAND OF THE

SULAS

VAMPIRE HILLS

VAMPIRE CITY

CAVE

ISLES of RA

N'LONGA'S VILLAGE

ZUNNAS VILLAGE

BASTI D

SLAVE COAST

KIRK

The World of
<u>SOLOMON KANE</u>
by J. Ramsey Campbell

The latter years of the sixteenth century were times of voyaging, of discovery, of men and exploits that became legend. The known world was growing; Cortez had discovered and destroyed the Aztec nation, Pizarro had conquered the Incas, Hernando de Soto had reached the Mississippi. Much of the world was still unknown, and many felt its call.

These were also years of religious strife. In France during 1572, fifty thousand Huguenots were massacred for their faith; in Spain, the Inquisition dealt out torture and death. Clearly, it was an age of fanaticism.

Injustice and exploitation were, as always, widespread. Spain looted the South American civilizations, but her treasure ships were themselves looted by the English in acts of piracy. The people of the West Indies were exploited; African Negroes were enslaved, with the approval of the church. Elsewhere, too, poverty flourished. Even in 1619, children were dying of cold in the London streets. In England, corrupt towns and neighborhoods in decay were common, as was idleness; work was regarded as a consequence of the Fall, and hence not to be thought of as honorable.

Is it any wonder that a Robert E. Howard character emerged?

It may seem curious that Solomon Kane was a Puritan. After all, weren't the Puritans of that time dour men who spent their lives objecting to details of church practice and disapproving of other people's pleasures? Surely no Puritan ever resembled Kane?

Perhaps not exactly, but it seems to me that many noted Puritans had it in them to be Kane. Consider Richard Norwood, author of a journal written in 1639–40. He had run away to sea, soldiered in the Netherlands, voyaged in the Mediterranean, and associated with Sir Henry Mainwaring, who shortly turned pirate. He had been shipwrecked, and attacked by pirates; he had suffered plague and imprisonment. His journeyings have been described as a "physical search for celestial happiness." If this sounds more peaceful than Kane's incessant wandering in search of or in pursuit of evil, Norwood shared at least one crucial trait with him: he suffered from paranoia, a diagnosis which Howard frequently applies to Kane.

In Norwood's case it turned inward; once, in the street, "all things seemed in their kinds to be my enemies. . . . It seemed then to my apprehension to proceed from indignation, wrath, and as it were a gnashing of teeth against me." If his condition had turned outward, how like Kane might he have become?

Many famous Puritans have been discussed as pathological cases, not least John Bunyan. But this underlines their courage rather than detracts from it—in Howard's tales as much as in reality, Kane has the great courage to trust his instincts. "A true fanatic," Howard writes of him in Red Shadows, "his promptings were reasons enough for his actions."

Also worth noting is the fact that the name of Puritan covered many—dare one say sins? Some thought that the word had been invented by "papists and atheists" as a pejorative term for their enemies. Its most generally agreed meaning, at least in the seventeenth century, referred to those who wanted to reform the Church of England from within; but some commentators feel that before 1620, it meant a "church rebel." Individual Puritans have been shown to be gamblers, and in a play of 1605, *Eastward Hoe*, Puritans are said to be "the smoothest and slickest knaves in a country." In any case, Howard writes of Kane (again in *Red Shadows*) that he "was not wholly a Puritan, though he thought of himself as such."

Perhaps all that one can say with certainty of Kane's background is that Puritanism, for most of its adherents, was a compulsion. Often it led to rational statements of the creed—Puritan autobiographies were common—but conversions to the faith were the result of terrifying visions, of harrowing self-examination, of paranoia and, frequently, hallucinations. No wonder Kane journeyed obsessively in search of something he could not define. The Puritan faith consisted of "knowing, feeling, and obeying the truth"; and these stories relate Kane's behavior under that compulsion, which is also his neverending search for some truth.

So much for Kane's conjectured background. Let Howard introduce the character; it is not the job of this introduction to rob anyone of meeting Kane in Howard's words. A few comments on the likely chronology of the stories—deduced by Glenn Lord from clues in the tales and in Howard's letters—may be useful.

Howard himself said, "Solomon Kane I created when I was in high school, at the age of about sixteen, but . . . several years passed before I put him on paper. He was probably the result of an admiration for a certain type of cold, steely-nerved duellist that existed in the sixteenth century."

It seems probable that "Skulls in the Stars" takes place around 1560. Already he has seen the Spanish Inquisition, though no tale chronicles this encounter. "The Right Hand of Doom" finds him still near Torkertown in England. But he finds it "hard to remain in the land of my birth for more than a month at a time." In *Red Shadows* (the first published Kane story, which appeared in the August 1928 *Weird Tales* as "Solomon Kane"), we discover him in France. Perhaps in the interim he has been "a captain in the French army for a space." His pursuit of evil takes him from France to Africa.

From Africa he sets sail again, and we hear nothing of him until he appears in the Black Forest in "Rattle of Bones." Perhaps meanwhile he has sailed with Sir Francis Drake, and has had the encounter described in "The One Black Stain"; in the next Black Forest story, "The Castle of the Devil," he has certainly been to sea. He returns to England, and a dying man's words send him on a search that lasts years, leading him eventually to the west coast of Africa and beyond, to the city of "The Moon of Skulls."

Only the opening pages of "The Castle of the Devil" survive. This Howard fragment appears here verbatim, and I have added what I hope is an appropriate development. I hope you will enjoy these tales as much as I enjoyed rereading them and adding my small contribution.

#1
SOLOMON KANE

Skulls in the Stars

SKULLS IN THE STARS

*He told how murders walk the earth
    Beneath the curse of Cain,
With crimson clouds before their eyes
    And flames about their brains:
For blood has left upon their souls
    Its everlasting stain.*

—Hood

I

There are two roads to Torkertown. One, the shorter and more direct route, leads across a barren upland moor, and the other, which is much longer, winds its tortuous way in and out among the hummocks and quagmires of the swamps, skirting the low hills to the east. It was a dangerous and tedious trail; so Solomon Kane halted in amazement when a breathless youth from the village he had just left, overtook him and implored him for God's sake to take the swamp road.

"The swamp road!" Kane stared at the boy.

He was a tall, gaunt man, was Solomon Kane, his darkly pallid face and deep brooding eyes made more somber by the drab Puritanical garb he affected.

"Yes, sir, 'tis far safer," the youngster answered to his surprised exclamation.

"Then the moor road must be haunted by Satan himself, for your townsmen warned me against traversing the other."

"Because of the quagmires, sir, that you might not see in the dark. You had better return to the village and continue your journey in the morning, sir."

"Taking the swamp road?"

"Yes, sir."

Kane shrugged his shoulders and shook his head.

"The moon rises almost as soon as twilight dies. By its light I can reach Torkertown in a few hours, across the moor."

"Sir, you had better not. No one ever goes that way. There are no houses at all upon the moor, while in the swamp there is the house of old Ezra who lives there all alone since his maniac cousin, Gideon, wandered off and died in the swamp and was never found —and old Ezra though a miser would not refuse you lodging should you decide to stop until morning. Since you must go, you had better go the swamp road."

Kane eyed the boy piercingly. The lad squirmed and shuffled his feet.

"Since this moor road is so dour to wayfarers," said the Puritan, "why did not the villagers tell me the whole tale, instead of vague mouthings?"

"Men like not to talk of it, sir. We hoped that you would take the swamp road after the men advised you to, but when we watched and saw that you turned not at the forks, they sent me to run after you and beg you to reconsider."

"Name of the Devil!" exclaimed Kane sharply, the unaccustomed oath showing his irritation; "the swamp road and the moor road—what is it that threatens me and why should I go miles out of my way and risk the bogs and mires?"

"Sir," said the boy, dropping his voice and drawing closer, "we be simple villagers who like not to talk of such things lest foul fortune befall us, but the moor road is a way accurst and hath not been traversed by any of the countryside for a year or more. It is death to walk those moors by night, as hath been found by some score of unfortunates. Some foul horror haunts the way and claims men for his victims."

"So? And what is this thing like?"

"No man knows. None has ever seen it and lived, but late-farers have heard terrible laughter far out on the fen and men have heard the horrid shrieks of its victims. Sir, in God's name return to the village, there pass the night, and tomorrow take the swamp trail to Torkertown."

Far back in Kane's gloomy eyes a scintillant light had begun to glimmer, like a witch's torch glinting under fathoms of cold gray ice. His blood quickened. Adventure! The lure of life-risk and drama! Not that Kane recognized his sensations as such. He sincerely considered that he voiced his real feelings when he said:

"These things be deeds of some power of evil. The lords of darkness have laid a curse upon the country. A strong man is needed to combat Satan and his might. Therefore I go, who have defied him many a time."

"Sir," the boy began, then closed his mouth as he saw the futility of argument. He only added, "The corpses of the victims are bruised and torn, sir."

He stood there at the crossroads, sighing regretfully as he watched the tall, rangy figure swinging up the road that led toward the moors.

The sun was setting as Kane came over the brow of the low hill which debouched into the upland fen. Huge and blood-red it sank down behind the sullen horizon of the moors, seeming to touch the rank grass with fire; so for a moment the watcher seemed to be gazing out across a sea of blood. Then the dark shadows came gliding from the east, the western blaze faded, and Solomon Kane struck out boldly in the gathering darkness.

The road was dim from disuse but was clearly defined. Kane went swiftly but warily, sword and pistols at hand. Stars blinked out and night winds whispered among the grass like weeping specters. The moon began to rise, lean and haggard, like a skull among the stars.

Then suddenly Kane stopped short. From somewhere in front of him sounded a strange and eery echo —or something like an echo. Again, this time louder.

Kane started forward again. Were his senses deceiving him? No!

Far out, there pealed a whisper of frightful laughter. And again, closer this time. No human being ever laughed like that—there was no mirth in it, only hatred and horror and soul-destroying terror. Kane halted. He was not afraid, but for the second he was almost unnerved. Then, stabbing through that awesome laughter, came the sound of a scream that was undoubtedly human. Kane started forward, increasing his gait. He cursed the illusive lights and flickering shadows which veiled the moor in the rising moon and made accurate sight impossible. The laughter continued, growing louder, as did the screams. Then sounded faintly the drum of frantic human feet. Kane broke into a run.

Some human was being hunted to death out there on the fen, and by what manner of horror God only knew. The sound of the flying feet halted abruptly and the screaming rose unbearably, mingled with other sounds unnamable and hideous. Evidently the man had been overtaken, and Kane, his flesh crawling, visualized some ghastly fiend of the darkness crouching on the back of its victim—crouching and tearing.

Then the noise of a terrible and short struggle came clearly through the abysmal silence of the night and the footfalls began again, but stumbling and uneven. The screaming continued, but with a gasping gurgle. The sweat stood cold on Kane's forehead and body. This was heaping horror on horror in an intolerable manner.

God, for a moment's clear light! The frightful drama was being enacted within a very short distance of him, to judge by the ease with which the sounds reached him. But this hellish half-light veiled all in shifting shadows, so that the moors appeared a haze of blurred illusions, and stunted trees and bushes seemed like giants.

Kane shouted, striving to increase the speed of his advance. The shrieks of the unknown broke into a hideous shrill squealing; again there was the sound of a struggle, and then from the shadows of the tall grass a thing came reeling—a thing that had once been a man—a gore-covered, frightful thing that fell at Kane's feet and writhed and groveled and raised its terrible face to the rising moon, and gibbered and yammered, and fell down again and died in its own blood.

The moon was up now and the light was better. Kane bent above the body, which lay stark in its unnamable mutilation, and he shuddered—a rare thing for him, who had seen the deeds of the Spanish Inquisition and the witch-finders.

Some wayfarer, he supposed. Then like a hand of ice on his spine he was aware that he was not alone. He looked up, his cold eyes piercing the shadows whence the dead man had staggered. He saw nothing, but he knew—he felt—that other eyes gave back his stare, terrible eyes not of this earth. He straightened and drew a pistol, waiting. The moonlight spread like a lake of pale blood over the moor, and trees and grasses took on their proper sizes.

The shadows melted, and Kane saw! At first he thought it only a shadow of mist, a wisp of moor fog that swayed in the tall grass before him. He gazed. More illusion, he thought. Then the thing began to take on shape, vague and indistinct. Two hideous eyes flamed at him—eyes which held all the stark horror which has been the heritage of man since the fearful dawn ages—eyes frightful and insane, with an insanity transcending earthly insanity. The form of the thing was misty and vague, a brain-shattering travesty on the human form, like, yet horribly unlike. The grass and bushes beyond showed clearly through it.

Kane felt the blood pound in his temples, yet he was as cold as ice. How such an unstable being as that which wavered before him could harm a man in a physical way was more than he could understand, yet the red horror at his feet gave mute testimony that the fiend could act with terrible material effect.

Of one thing Kane was sure: there would be no hunting of him across the dreary moors, no screaming and fleeing to be dragged down again and again. If he must die he would die in his tracks, his wounds in front.

Now a vague and grisly mouth gaped wide and the demoniac laughter again shrieked but, soul-shaking in its nearness. And in the midst of that threat of doom, Kane deliberately leveled his long pistol and fired. A maniacal yell of rage and mockery answered the report, and the thing came at him like a flying sheet of smoke, long shadowy arms stretched to drag him down.

Kane, moving with the dynamic speed of a famished wolf, fired the second pistol with as little effect, snatched his long rapier from its sheath and thrust into the center of the misty attacker. The blade sang as it passed clear through, encountering no solid resistance, and Kane felt icy fingers grip his limbs, bestial talons tear his garments and the skin beneath.

He dropped the useless sword and sought to grapple with his foe. It was like fighting a floating mist, a flying shadow armed with daggerlike claws. His savage blows met empty air, his leanly mighty arms, in whose grasp strong men had died, swept nothingness and clutched emptiness. Naught was solid or real save the flaying, ape-like fingers with their crooked talons, and the crazy eyes which burned into the shuddering depths of his soul.

Kane realized that he was in a desperate plight indeed. Already his garments hung in tatters and he bled from a score of deep wounds. But he never flinched, and the thought of flight never entered his mind. He had never fled from a single foe, and had the thought occurred to him he would have flushed with shame.

He saw no help for it now, but that his form should lie there beside the fragments of the other victim, but the thought held no terrors for him. His only wish was to give as good an account of himself as possible before the end came, and if he could, to inflict some damage on his unearthly foe.

There above the dead man's torn body, man fought with demon under the pale light of the rising moon, with all the advantages with the demon, save one. And that one was enough to overcome all the others. For if abstract hate may bring into material substance a ghostly thing, may not courage, equally abstract, form a concrete weapon to combat that ghost?

Kane fought with his arms and his feet and his hands, and he was aware at last that the ghost began to give back before him, and the fearful laughter changed to screams of baffled fury. For man's only weapon is courage that flinches not from the gates of Hell itself, and against such not even the legions of Hell can stand.

Of this Kane knew nothing; he only knew that the talons which tore and rended him seemed to grow weaker and wavering, that a wild light grew and grew in the horrible eyes. And reeling and gasping, he rushed in, grappled the thing at last and threw it, and as they tumbled about on the moor and it writhed and lapped his limbs like a serpent of smoke, his flesh crawled and his hair stood on end, for he began to understand its gibbering.

He did not hear and comprehend as a man hears and comprehends the speech of a man, but the frightful secrets it imparted in whisperings and yammerings and screaming silences sank fingers of ice into his soul, and he *knew*.

II

The hut of old Ezra the miser stood by the road in the midst of the swamp, half screened by the sullen trees which grew about it. The walls were rotting, the roof crumbling, and great, pallid and green fungus-monsters clung to it and writhed about the doors and windows, as if seeking to peer within. The trees leaned above it and their gray branches intertwined so that it crouched in semi-darkness like a monstrous dwarf over whose shoulder ogres leer.

The road which wound down into the swamp, among rotting stumps and rank hummocks and scummy, snake-haunted pools and bogs, crawled past the hut. Many people passed that way these days, but few saw old Ezra, save a glimpse of a yellow face, peering through the fungus-screened windows, itself like an ugly fungus.

Old Ezra the miser partook much of the quality of the swamp, for he was gnarled and bent and sullen; his fingers were like clutching parasitic plants and his locks hung like drab moss above eyes trained to the murk of the swamplands. His eyes were like a dead man's, yet hinted of depths abysmal and loathsome as the dead lakes of the swamplands.

These eyes gleamed now at the man who stood in front of his hut. This man was tall and gaunt and dark, his face was haggard and claw-marked, and he was bandaged of arm and leg. Somewhat behind this man stood a number of villagers.

"You are Ezra of the swamp road?"

"Aye, and what want ye of me?"

"Where is your cousin Gideon, the maniac youth who abode with you?"

"Gideon?"

"Aye."

"He wandered away into the swamp and never came back. No doubt he lost his way and was set upon by wolves or died in a quagmire or was struck by an adder."

"How long ago?"

"Over a year."

"Aye. Hark ye, Ezra the miser. Soon after your cousin's disappearance, a countryman, coming home across the moors, was set upon by some unknown fiend and torn to pieces, and thereafter it became death to cross those moors. First men of the countryside, then strangers who wandered over the fen, fell to the clutches of the thing. Many men have died, since the first one.

"Last night I crossed the moors, and heard the flight and pursuing of another victim, a stranger who knew not the evil of the moors. Ezra the miser, it was a fearful thing, for the wretch twice broke from the fiend, terribly wounded, and each time the demon caught and dragged him down again. And at last he fell dead at my very feet, done to death in a manner that would freeze the statue of a saint."

The villagers moved restlessly and murmured fearfully to each other, and old Ezra's eyes shifted furtively. Yet the somber expression of Solomon Kane never altered, and his condor-like stare seemed to transfix the miser.

"Aye, aye!" muttered old Ezra hurriedly; "a bad thing, a bad thing! Yet why do you tell this thing to me?"

"Aye, a sad thing. Harken further, Ezra. The fiend came out of the shadows and I fought with it, over the body of its victim. Aye, how I overcame it, I know not, for the battle was hard and long, but the powers of good and light were on my side, which are mightier than the powers of Hell.

"At the last I was stronger, and it broke from me and fled, and I followed to no avail. Yet before it fled it whispered to me a monstrous truth."

Old Ezra started, stared wildly, seemed to shrink into himself.

"Nay, why tell me this?" he muttered.

"I returned to the village and told my tale," said Kane, "for I knew that now I had the power to rid the moors of their curse forever. Ezra, come with us!"

"Where?" gasped the miser.

To the rotting oak on the moors.

Ezra reeled as though struck; he screamed incoherently and turned to flee.

On the instant, at Kane's sharp order, two brawny villagers sprang forward and seized the miser. They twisted the dagger from his withered hand, and pinioned his arms, shuddering as their fingers encountered his clammy flesh.

Kane motioned them to follow, and turning strode up the trail, followed by the villagers, who found their strength taxed to the utmost in their task of bearing their prisoner along. Through the swamp they went and out, taking a little-used trail which led up over the low hills and out on the moors.

The sun was sliding down the horizon and old Ezra stared at it with bulging eyes—stared as if he could not gaze enough. Far out on the moors reared up the great oak tree, like a gibbet, now only a decaying shell. There Solomon Kane halted.

Old Ezra writhed in his captor's grasp and made inarticulate noises.

"Over a year ago," said Solomon Kane, "you, fearing that your insane cousin Gideon would tell men of your cruelties to him, brought him away from the swamp by the very trail by which we came, and murdered him here in the night."

Ezra cringed and snarled.

"You can not prove this lie!"

Kane spoke a few words to an agile villager. The youth clambered up the rotting bole of the tree and from a crevice, high up, dragged something that fell with a clatter at the feet of the miser. Ezra went limp with a terrible shriek.

The object was a man's skeleton, the skull cleft.

"You—how knew you this? You are Satan!" gibbered old Ezra.

Kane folded his arms.

"The thing I fought last night told me this thing as we reeled in battle, and I followed it to this tree. *For the fiend is Gideon's ghost.*"

Ezra shrieked again and fought savagely.

"You knew," said Kane somberly, "you knew what

thing did these deeds. You feared the ghost of the maniac, and that is why you chose to leave his body on the fen instead of concealing it in the swamp. For you knew the ghost would haunt the place of his death. He was insane in life, and in death he did not know where to find his slayer; else he had come to you in your hut. He hates no man but you, but his mazed spirit can not tell one man from another, and he slays all, lest he let his killer escape. Yet he will know you and rest in peace forever after. Hate hath made of his ghost a solid thing that can rend and slay, and though he feared you terribly in life, in death he fears you not at all."

Kane halted. He glanced at the sun.

"All this I had from Gideon's ghost, in his yammerings and his whisperings and his shrieking silences. Naught but your death will lay that ghost."

Ezra listened in breathless silence and Kane pronounced the words of his doom.

"A hard thing it is," said Kane somberly, "to sentence a man to death in cold blood and in such a manner as I have in mind, but you must die that others may live—and God knoweth you deserve death.

"You shall not die by noose, bullet or sword, but at the talons of him you slew—for naught else will satiate him."

At these words Ezra's brain shattered, his knees gave way and he fell groveling and screaming for death, begging them to burn him at the stake, to flay him alive. Kane's face was set like death, and the the villagers, the fear rousing their cruelty, bound the screeching wretch to the oak tree, and one of them bade him make his peace with God. But Ezra made no answer, shrieking in a high shrill voice with unbearable monotony. Then the villager would have struck the miser across the face, but Kane stayed him.

"Let him make his peace with Satan, whom he is more like to meet," said the Puritan grimly. "The sun is about to set. Loose his cords so that he may work loose by dark, since it is better to meet death free and unshackled than bound like a sacrifice."

As they turned to leave him, old Ezra yammered and gibbered unhuman sounds and then fell silent, staring at the sun with terrible intensity.

They walked away across the fen, and Kane flung a last look at the grotesque form bound to the tree, seeming in the uncertain light like a great fungus growing to the bole. And suddenly the miser screamed hideously:

"Death! Death! There are skulls in the stars!"

"Life was good to him, though he was gnarled and churlish and evil," Kane sighed. "Mayhap God has a place for such souls where fire and sacrifice may cleanse them of their dross as fire cleans the forest of fungus things. Yet my heart is heavy within me."

"Nay, sir," one of the villagers spoke, "you have done but the will of God, and good alone shall come of this night's deed."

"Nay," answered Kane heavily. "I know not—I know not."

The sun had gone down and night spread with amazing swiftness, as if great shadows came rushing down from unknown voids to cloak the world with hurrying darkness. Through the thick night came a weird echo, and the men halted and looked back the way they had come.

Nothing could be seen. The moor was an ocean of shadows and the tall grass about them bent in long waves before the faint wind, breaking the deathly stillness with breathless murmurings.

Then far away the red disk of the moon rose over the fen, and for an instant a grim silhouette was etched blackly against it. A shape came flying across the face of the moon—a bent, grotesque thing whose feet seemed scarcely to touch the earth; and close behind came a thing like a flying shadow—a nameless, shapeless horror.

A moment the racing twain stood out boldly against the moon; then they merged into one unnamable, formless mass, and vanished in the shadows.

Far across the fen sounded a single shriek of terrible laughter.

THE RIGHT HAND OF DOOM

"And he hangs at dawn! Ho! Ho!"

The speaker smote his thigh resoundingly and laughed in a high-pitched grating voice. He glanced boastfully at his hearers, and gulped the wine which stood at his elbow. The fire leaped and flickered in the tap-room fireplace and no one answered him.

"Roger Simeon, the necromancer!" sneered the grating voice, "a dealer in the diabolic arts and a worker of black magic! My word, all his foul power could not save him when the king's soldiers surrounded his cave and took him prisoner. He fled when the people began to fling cobble stones at his windows, and thought to hide himself and escape to France. Ho! Ho! His escape shall be at the end of a noose. A good day's work, say I."

He tossed a small bag on the table where it clinked musically.

"The price of a magician's life!" he boasted. "What say you, my sour friend?"

This last was addressed to a tall silent man who sat near the fire. This man, gaunt, powerful and somberly dressed, turned his darkly pallid face toward the speaker and fixed him with a pair of deep icy eyes.

"I say," said he in a low powerful voice, "that you have this day done a damnable deed. Yon necromancer was worthy of death, belike, but he trusted you, naming you his one friend, and you betrayed him for a few filthy coins. Methinks you will meet him in Hell, some day."

14

The first speaker, a short, stocky and evil-faced
fellow, opened his mouth as if for an angry retort and
then hesitated. The icy eyes held his for an instant,
then the tall man rose with a smooth cat-like motion
and strode from the tap room in long springy strides.

"Who is yon?" asked the boaster resentfully. "Who
is he to uphold magicians against honest men? By
God, he is lucky to cross words with John Redly and
keep his heart in's bosom!"

The tavern-keeper leaned forward to secure an
ember for his long-stemmed pipe and answered dryly:

"And you be lucky too, John, for keepin' tha' mouth
shut. That be Solomon Kane, the Puritan, a man
dangerouser than a wolf."

Redly grumbled beneath his breath, muttered an
oath, and sullenly replaced the money bag in his belt.

"Are ye stayin' here tonight?"

"Aye," Redly answered sullenly. "Rather I'd stay
to watch Simeon hang in Torkertown tomorrow, but
I'm London bound at dawn."

The tavern-keeper filled their goblets.

"Here's to Simeon's soul, God ha' mercy on the
wretch, and may he fail in the vengeance he swore to
take on you."

John Redly started, swore, then laughed with reckless bravado. The laughter rose emptily and broke on
a false note.

Solomon Kane awoke suddenly and sat up in bed.
He was a light sleeper as becomes a man who habit-
ually carries his life in his hand. And somewhere in
the house had sounded a noise which had roused him.
He listened. Outside, as he could see through the
shutters, the world was whitening with the first tints
of dawn.

Suddenly the sound came again, faintly. It was as
if a cat were clawing its way up the wall, outside.
Kane listened, and then came a sound as if someone
were fumbling at the shutters. The Puritan rose, and
sword in hand, crossed the room suddenly and flung

them open. The world lay sleeping to his gaze. A late moon hovered over the western horizon. No marauder lurked outside his window. He leaned out, gazing at the window of the chamber next his. The shutters were open.

Kane closed his shutters and crossed to his door; went out into the corridor. He was acting on impulse as he usually did. These were wild times. This tavern was some miles from the nearest town—Torkertown. Bandits were common. Someone or something had entered the chamber next his, and its sleeping occupant might be in danger. Kane did not halt to weigh pros and cons but went straight to the chamber door and opened it.

The window was wide open and the light, streaming in, illumined the room yet made it seem to swim in a ghostly mist. A man snored on the bed and he Kane recognized as John Redly, the man who had betrayed the necromancer to the soldiers.

Then his gaze was drawn to the window. On the sill squatted what looked like a huge spider, and as Kane watched, it dropped to the floor and began to crawl toward the bed. The thing was broad and hairy and dark, and Kane noted that it had left a stain on the window sill. It moved on five thick and curiously jointed legs and altogether had such an eery appearance about it that Kane was spellbound for the moment. Now it had reached Redly's bed and clambered up the bedstead in a strange clumsy sort of manner.

Now it poised directly over the sleeping man, clinging to the bedstead, and Kane started forward with a shout of warning. That instant Redly awoke and looked up. His eyes flared wide, a terrible scream broke from his lips and simultaneously the spider-thing dropped, landing full on his neck. And even as Kane reached the bed, he saw the legs lock and heard the splintering of John Redly's neck bones. The man stiffened and lay still, his head lolling grotesquely on his broken neck. And the thing dropped from him and lay limply on the bed.

Kane bent over the grim spectacle, scarcely believing his eyes. For the thing which had opened the shutters, crawled across the floor and murdered John Redly in his bed was a *human hand!*

Now it lay flaccid and lifeless. And Kane gingerly thrust his rapier point through it and lifted it to his eyes. The hand was that of a large man, apparently, for it was broad and thick, with heavy fingers, and was almost covered by a matted growth of ape-like hair. It had been severed at the wrist and was caked with blood. A thin silver ring was on the second finger, a curious ornament, made in the form of a coiling serpent.

Kane stood gazing at the hideous relic as the tavern-keeper entered, clad in his night shirt, candle in one hand and blunderbuss in the other.

"What's this?" he roared as his eyes fell on the corpse on the bed.

Then he saw what Kane held spitted on his sword and his face went white. As if drawn by an irresistible urge, he came closer—his eyes bulged. Then he reeled back and sank into a chair, so pale Kane thought he was going to swoon.

"God's name, sir," he gasped. "Let that thing not live! There be a fire in the tap room, sir—"

Kane came into Torkertown before the morning had waned. At the outskirts of the village he met a garrulous youth who hailed him.

"Sir, like all honest men you will be pleasured to know that Roger Simeon the black magician was hanged this dawn, just as the sun came up."

"And was his passing manly?" asked Kane somberly.

"Aye, sir, he flinched not, but a weird deed it was. Look ye, sir, Roger Simeon went to the gallows with but one hand to his arms!"

"And how came that about?"

"Last night, sir, as he sat in his cell like a great black spider, he called one of his guards and asking for a last favor, bade the soldier strike off his right hand! The man would not do it at first, but he feared Roger's curse, and at last he took his sword and smote off the hand at the wrist. Then Simeon, taking it in his left hand, flung it far through the bars of his cell window, uttering many strange and foul words of magic. The guards were sore afraid, but Roger offered not to harm them, saying he hated only John Redly that betrayed him.

"And he bound the stump of his arm to stop the blood and all the rest of the night he sat as a man in a trance and at times he mumbled to himself as a man that unknowing, talks to himself. And, 'To the right,' he would whisper, and 'Bear to the left!' and, 'On, on!'

"Oh, sir, 'twas grisly to hear him, they say, and to see him crouching over the bloody stump of his arm! And as dawn was gray they came and took him forth to the gallows and as they placed the noose about his neck, sudden he writhed and strained as with terrible effort, and the muscles in his right arm which lacked the hand, bulged and creaked as though he were breaking some mortal's neck!

"Then as the guards sprang to seize him, he ceased and began to laugh, and terrible and hideous his laughter bellowed out until the noose broke it short and he hung black and silent in the red eye of the rising sun."

Solomon Kane was silent for he was thinking of the fearful terror which had twisted John Redly's features in that last swift moment of awakening and life, ere doom struck. And a dim picture rose in his mind— that of a hairy severed hand crawling on its fingers like a great spider, blindly, through the dark nighttime forests to scale a wall and fumble open a pair of bedroom shutters. Here his vision stopped, recoiling from the continuance of that dark and bloody drama. What terrible fires of hate had blazed in the soul of the doomed necromancer and what hideous powers had been his, to so send that bloody hand groping on its mission, guided by the magic and will of that burning brain!

Yet to make sure, Solomon asked:

"And was the hand ever found?"

"Nay sir. Men found the place where it had fallen when it was thrown from the cell, but it was gone, and a trail of red led into the forest. Doubtless a wolf devoured it."

"Doubtless," answered Solomon Kane. "And were Roger Simeon's hands great and hairy with a ring on the second finger of the right hand?"

"Aye, sir. A silver ring coiled like unto a snake."

RED SHADOWS

CHAPTER 1

THE COMING OF SOLOMON

The moonlight shimmered hazily, making silvery mists
of illusion among the shadowy trees. A faint breeze
whispered down the valley, bearing a shadow that was
not of the moon-mist. A faint scent of smoke was
apparent.

The man whose long, swinging strides, unhurried
yet unswerving, had carried him for many a mile since
sunrise, stopped suddenly. A movement in the trees
had caught his attention, and he moved silently toward
the shadows, a hand resting lightly on the hilt of his
long, slim rapier.

Warily he advanced, his eyes striving to pierce the
darkness that brooded under the trees. This was a
wild and menacing country; death might be lurking
under those trees. Then his hand fell away from the
hilt and he leaned forward. Death indeed was there,
but not in such shape as might cause him fear.

"The fires of Hades!" he murmured. "A girl! What
has harmed you, child? Be not afraid of me."

The girl looked up at him, her face like a dim white
rose in the dark.

"You—who are—you?" her words came in gasps.

"Naught but a wanderer, a landless man, but a friend
to all in need." The gentle voice sounded somehow
incongruous, coming from the man.

The girl sought to prop herself up on her elbow,
and instantly he knelt and raised her to a sitting posi-

20

tion, her head resting against his shoulder. His hand touched her breast and came away red and wet.

"Tell me." His voice was soft, soothing, as one speaks to a babe.

"Le Loup," she gasped, her voice swiftly growing weaker. "He and his men—descended upon our village—a mile up the valley. They robbed—slew— burned—"

"That, then, was the smoke I scented," muttered the man. "Go on, child."

"I ran. He, the Wolf, pursued me—and—caught me—" The words died away in a shuddering silence.

"I understand, child. Then—?"

"Then—he—he—stabbed me—with his dagger— oh, blessed saints!—mercy—"

Suddenly the slim form went limp. The man eased her to the earth, and touched her brow lightly.

"Dead!" he muttered.

Slowly he rose, mechanically wiping his hands upon his cloak. A dark scowl had settled on his somber brow. Yet he made no wild, reckless vow, swore no oath by saints or devils.

"Men shall die for this," he said coldly.

CHAPTER 2
THE LAIR OF THE WOLF

"You are a fool!" The words came in a cold snarl that curdled the hearer's blood.

He who had just been named a fool lowered his eyes sullenly without answer.

"You and all the others I lead!" The speaker leaned forward, his fist pounding emphasis on the rude table between them. He was a tall, rangy-built man, supple as a leopard and with a lean, cruel, predatory face. His eyes danced and glittered with a kind of reckless mockery.

The fellow spoken to replied sullenly, "This Solomon Kane is a demon from Hell, I tell you."

"Faugh! Dolt! He is a man—who will die from a pistol ball or a sword thrust."

"So thought Jean, Juan and La Costa," answered the other grimly. "Where are they? Ask the mountain wolves that tore the flesh from their dead bones. Where does this Kane hide? We have searched the mountains and the valleys for leagues, and we have found no trace. I tell you, Le Loup, he comes up from Hell. I knew no good would come from hanging that friar a moon ago."

The Wolf strummed impatiently upon the table. His keen face, despite lines of wild living and dissipation, was the face of a thinker. The superstitions of his followers affected him not at all.

"Faugh! I say again. The fellow has found some cavern or secret vale of which we do not know where he hides in the day."

"And at night he sallies forth and slays us," gloomily commented the other. "He hunts us down as a wolf hunts deer—by God, Le Loup, you name yourself Wolf but I think you have met at last a fiercer and more crafty wolf than yourself! The first we know of this man is when we find Jean, the most desperate bandit unhung, nailed to a tree with his own dagger through his breast, and the letters S. L. K. carved upon his dead cheeks.

"Then the Spaniard Juan is struck down, and after we find him he lives long enough to tell us that his slayer is an Englishman, Solomon Kane, who has sworn to destroy our entire band! What then? La Costa, a swordsman second only to yourself, goes forth swearing to meet this Kane. By the demons of perdition, it seems he met him! For we found his sword-pierced corpse upon a cliff. What now? Are we all to fall before this English fiend?"

"True, our best men have been done to death by him," mused the bandit chief. "Soon the rest return from that little trip to the hermit's; then we shall see. Kane can not hide forever. Then—ha, what was that?"

The two turned swiftly as a shadow fell across the table. Into the entrance of the cave that formed the bandit lair, a man staggered. His eyes were wide and staring; he reeled on buckling legs, and a dark red stain dyed his tunic. He came a few tottering steps forward, then pitched across the table, sliding off onto the floor.

"Hell's devils!" cursed the Wolf, hauling him upright and propping him in a chair. "Where are the rest, curse you?"

"Dead! All dead!"

"How? Satan's curses on you, speak!" The Wolf shook the man savagely, the other bandit gazing on in wide-eyed horror.

"We reached the hermit's hut just as the moon rose," the man muttered. "I stayed outside—to watch —the others went in—to torture the hermit—to make him reveal—the hiding place—of his gold."

"Yes, yes! Then what?" The Wolf was raging with impatience.

"Then the world turned red—the hut went up in a roar and a red rain flooded the valley—through it I saw—the hermit and a tall man clad all in black— coming from the trees—"

"Solomon Kane!" gasped the bandit. "I knew it! I—"

"Silence, fool!" snarled the chief. "Go on!"

"I fled—Kane pursued—wounded me—but I outran—him—got—here—first—"

The man slumped forward on the table.

"Saints and devils!" raged the Wolf. "What does he look like, this Kane?"

"Like—Satan—"

The voice trailed off in silence. The dead man slid from the table to lie in a red heap upon the floor.

"Like Satan!" babbled the other bandit. "I told you! 'Tis the Horned One himself! I tell you—"

He ceased as a frightened face peered in at the cave entrance.

"Kane?"

"Aye." The Wolf was too much at sea to lie. "Keep close watch, La Mon; in a moment the Rat and I will join you."

The face withdrew and Le Loup turned to the other.

"This ends the band," said he. "You, I, and that thief La Mon are all that are left. What would you suggest?"

The Rat's pallid lips barely formed the word: "Flight!"

"You are right. Let us take the gems and gold from the chests and flee, using the secret passageway."

"And La Mon?"

"He can watch until we are ready to flee. Then— why divide the treasure three ways?"

A faint smile touched the Rat's malevolent features. Then a sudden thought smote him.

"He," indicating the corpse on the floor, "said, 'I got here first.' Does that mean Kane was pursuing him here?" And as the Wolf nodded impatiently the other turned to the chests with chattering haste.

The flickering candle on the rough table lighted up a strange and wild scene. The light, uncertain and dancing, gleamed redly in the slowly widening lake of blood in which the dead man lay; it danced upon the heaps of gems and coins emptied hastily upon the floor from the brass-bound chests that ranged the walls; and it glittered in the eyes of the Wolf with the same gleam which sparkled from his sheathed dagger.

The chests were empty, their treasure lying in a shimmering mass upon the blood-stained floor. The Wolf stopped and listened. Outside was silence. There was no moon, and Le Loup's keen imagination pictured the dark slayer, Solomon Kane, gliding through the blackness, a shadow among shadows. He grinned crookedly; this time the Englishman would be foiled.

"There is a chest yet unopened," said he, pointing.

The Rat, with a muttered exclamation of surprise, bent over the chest indicated. With a single, cat-like motion, the Wolf sprang upon him, sheathing his dagger to the hilt in the Rat's back, between the shoulders. The Rat sagged to the floor without a sound.

"Why divide the treasure two ways?" murmured Le Loup, wiping his blade upon the dead man's doublet. "Now for La Mon."

He stepped toward the door; then stopped and shrank back.

At first he thought it was the shadow of a man who stood in the entrance; then he saw that it was a man himself, though so dark and still he stood that a fantastic semblance of shadow was lent him by the glittering candle.

A tall man, as tall as Le Loup he was, clad in black from head to foot, in plain, close-fitting garments that somehow suited the somber face. Long arms and broad shoulders betokened the swordsman, as plainly as the long rapier in his hand. The features of the man were saturnine and gloomy. A kind of dark pallor lent him a ghostly appearance in the uncertain light, an effect heightened by the satanic darkness of his lowering brows.

Eyes, large, deep-set and unblinking, fixed their gaze upon the bandit, and looking into them, Le Loup was unable to decide what color they were. Strangely, the Mephistophelean trend of the lower features was offset by a high, broad forehead, though this was partly hidden by a featherless hat.

That forehead marked the dreamer, the idealist, the introvert, just as the eyes and the thin, straight nose betrayed the fanatic. An observer would have been struck by the eyes of the two men who stood there, facing each other. Eyes of both betokened untold deeps of power, but there the resemblance ceased.

The eyes of the bandit were hard, almost opaque, with a curious scintillant shallowness that reflected a thousand changing lights and gleams, like some strange gem; there was mockery in those eyes, cruelty and recklessness.

The eyes of the man in black, on the other hand, deep-set and staring from under prominent brows, were cold but deep; gazing into them, one had the impression of looking into countless fathoms of ice.

Now the eyes clashed, and the Wolf, who was used to being feared, felt a strange coolness on his spine. The sensation was new to him—a new thrill to one who lived for thrills, and he laughed suddenly.

"You are Solomon Kane, I suppose?" he asked, managing to make his question sound politely incurious.

"I am Solomon Kane." The voice was resonant and powerful. "Are you prepared to meet your God?"

"Why, Monsieur," Le Loup answered, bowing, "I assure you I am as ready as I ever will be. I might ask Monsieur the same question."

"No doubt I stated my inquiry wrongly," Kane said grimly. "I will change it: are you prepared to meet your master, the Devil?"

"As to that, Monsieur"—Le Loup examined his fingernails with elaborate unconcern—"I must say that I can at present render a most satisfactory account to his Horned Excellency, though really I have no intention of so doing—for awhile at least."

Le Loup did not wonder as to the fate of La Mon; Kane's presence in the cave was sufficient answer that did not need the trace of blood on his rapier to verify it.

"What I wish to know, Monsieur," said the bandit, "is why in the Devil's name have you harassed my band as you have, and how did you destroy that last set of fools?"

"Your last question is easily answered, sir," Kane replied. "I myself had the tale spread that the hermit possessed a store of gold, knowing that would draw your scum as carrion draws vultures.

"For days and nights I have watched the hut, and

tonight, when I saw your villains coming, I warned the hermit, and together we went among the trees back of the hut. Then, when the rogues were inside, I struck flint and steel to the trail I had laid, and flame ran through the trees like a red snake until it reached the powder I had placed beneath the hut floor. Then the hut and thirteen sinners went to Hell in a great roar of flame and smoke. True, one escaped, but him I had slain in the forest had not I stumbled and fallen upon a broken root, which gave him time to elude me."

"Monsieur," said Le Loup with another low bow, "I grant you the admiration I must needs bestow on a brave and shrewd foeman. Yet tell me this: Why have you followed me as a wolf follows deer?"

"Some moons ago," said Kane, his frown becoming more menacing, "you and your fiends raided a small village down the valley. You know the details better than I. There was a girl there, a mere child, who, hoping to escape your lust, fled up the valley; but you, you jackal of Hell, you caught her and left her, violated and dying. I found her there, and above her dead form I made up my mind to hunt you down and kill you."

"H'm," mused the Wolf. "Yes, I remember the wench. Mon Dieu, so the softer sentiments enter into the affair! Monsieur, I had not thought you an amorous man; be not jealous, good fellow, there are many more wenches."

"Le Loup, take care!" Kane exclaimed, a terrible menace in his voice. "I have never yet done a man to death by torture, but by God, sir, you tempt me!"

The tone, and more especially the unexpected oath, coming as it did from Kane, slightly sobered Le Loup; his eyes narrowed and his hand moved toward his rapier. The air was tense for an instant; then the Wolf relaxed elaborately.

"Who was the girl?" he asked idly. "Your wife?"

"I never saw her before," answered Kane.

"Nom d'un nom!" swore the bandit. "What sort of a man are you, Monsieur, who takes up a feud of this sort merely to avenge a wench unknown to you?"

"That, sir, is my own affair; it is sufficient that I do so."

Kane could not have explained, even to himself, nor did he ever seek an explanation within himself. A true fanatic, his promptings were reasons enough for his actions.

"You are right, Monsieur." Le Loup was sparring now for time; casually he edged backward inch by inch, with such consummate acting skill that he aroused no suspicion even in the hawk who watched him.

"Monsieur," he said, "possibly you will say that you are merely a noble cavalier, wandering about like a true Galahad, protecting the weaker; but you and I know different. There on the floor is the equivalent to an emperor's ransom. Let us divide it peaceably; then if you like not my company, why—nom d'un nom!—we can go our separate ways."

Kane leaned forward, a terrible brooding threat growing in his cold eyes. He seemed like a great condor about to launch himself upon his victim.

"Sir, do you assume me to be as great a villain as yourself?"

Suddenly Le Loup threw back his head, his eyes dancing and leaping with a mild mockery and a kind of insane recklessness. His shout of laughter sent the echoes flying.

"Gods of Hell! No, you fool, I do not class you with myself! Mon Dieu, Monsieur Kane, you have a task indeed if you intend to avenge all the wenches who have known my favors!"

"Shades of death! Shall I waste time in parleying with this base scoundrel" Kane snarled in a voice suddenly blood-thirsting, and his lean frame flashed forward like a bent bow suddenly released.

At the same instant Le Loup with a wild laugh

bounded backward with a movement as swift as Kane's. His timing was perfect; his back-flung hands struck the table and hurled it aside, plunging the cave into darkness as the candle toppled and went out.

Kane's rapier sang like an arrow in the dark as he thrust blindly and ferociously.

"Adieu, Monsieur Galahad!" the taunt came from somewhere in front of him, but Kane, plunging toward the sound with the savage fury of baffled wrath, caromed against a blank wall that did not yield to his blow. From somewhere seemed to come an echo of a mocking laugh.

Kane whirled, eyes fixed on the dimly outlined entrance, thinking his foe would try to slip past him and out of the cave; but no form bulked there, and when his groping hands found the candle and lighted it, the cave was empty, save for himself and the dead men on the floor.

CHAPTER 3
THE CHANT OF THE DRUMS

Across the dusky waters the whisper came: boom, boom, boom!—a sullen reiteration. Far away and more faintly sounded a whisper of different timbre: thrum, throom, thrum! Back and forth went the vibrations as the throbbing drums spoke to each other. What tales did they carry? What monstrous secrets whispered across the sullen, shadowy reaches of the unmapped jungle?

"This, you are sure, is the bay where the Spanish ship put in?"

"Yes, Senhor; the negro swears this is the bay where the white man left the ship alone and went into the jungle."

Kane nodded grimly.

"Then put me ashore here, alone. Wait seven days; then if I have not returned and if you have no word of me, set sail wherever you will."

"Yes, Senhor."

The waves slapped lazily against the sides of the boat that carried Kane ashore. The village that he sought was on the river bank but set back from the bay shore, the jungle hiding it from sight of the ship.

Kane had adopted what seemed the most hazardous course, that of going ashore by night, for the reason that he knew, if the man he sought were in the village, he would never reach it by day. As it was, he was taking a most desperate chance in daring the night-time jungle, but all his life he had been used to taking desperate chances. Now he gambled his life upon the slim chance of gaining the native village under cover of darkness and unknown to the villagers.

At the beach he left the boat with a few muttered commands, and as the rowers put back to the ship which lay anchored some distance out in the bay, he turned and engulfed himself in the blackness of the jungle. Sword in one hand, dagger in the other, he stole forward, seeking to keep pointed in the direction from which the drums still muttered and grumbled.

He went with the stealth and easy movement of a leopard, feeling his way cautiously, every nerve alert and straining, but the way was not easy.

Vines tripped him and slapped him in the face, impeding his progress; he was forced to grope his way between the huge boles of towering trees, and all through the underbrush about him sounded vague and menacing rustlings and shadows of movement. Thrice his foot touched something that moved beneath it and writhed away, and once he glimpsed the baleful glimmer of feline eyes among the trees. They vanished, however, as he advanced.

Thrum, thrum, thrum, came the ceaseless monotone of the drums: war and death (they said); blood and lust; human sacrifice and human feast! The soul of Africa (said the drums); the spirit of the jungle; the chant of the gods of outer darkness, the gods that roar and gibber, the gods men knew when dawns were young, beast-eyed, gaping-mouthed, huge-bellied, bloody-handed, the Black Gods (sang the drums).

All this and more the drums roared and bellowed to Kane as he worked his way through the forest. Somewhere in his soul a responsive chord was smitten and answered. You too are of the night (sang the drums); there is the strength of darkness, the strength of the primitive in you; come back down the ages; let us teach you, let us teach you (chanted the drums).

Kane stepped out of the thick jungle and came upon a plainly defined trail. Beyond, through the trees came the gleam of the village fires, flames glowing through the palisades. Kane walked down the trail swiftly.

He went silently and warily, sword extended in front of him, eyes straining to catch any hint of movement in the darkness ahead, for the trees loomed like sullen giants on each hand; sometimes their great branches intertwined above the trail and he could see only a slight way ahead of him.

Like a dark ghost he moved along the shadowed trail; alertly he stared and harkened; yet no warning came first to him, as a great, vague bulk rose up out of the shadows and struck him down, silently.

CHAPTER 4

THE BLACK GOD

Thrum, thrum, thrum! Somewhere, with deadening monotony, a cadence was repeated, over and over, bearing out the same theme: "Fool—fool—fool!" Now it was far away, now he could stretch out his hand and almost reach it. Now it merged with the throbbing in his head until the two vibrations were as one: "Fool—fool—fool—fool—"

The fogs faded and vanished. Kane sought to raise his hand to his head, but found that he was bound hand and foot. He lay on the floor of a hut—alone? He twisted about to view the place. No, two eyes glimmered at him from the darkness. Now a form took shape, and Kane, still mazed, believed that he looked on the man who had struck him unconscious. Yet no; this man could never strike such a blow. He was lean, withered and wrinkled. The only thing that seemed alive about him were his eyes, and they seemed like the eyes of a snake.

The man squatted on the floor of the hut, near the doorway, naked save for a loin-cloth and the usual paraphernalia of bracelets, anklets and armlets. Weird fetishes of ivory, bone and hide, animal and human, adorned his arms and legs. Suddenly and unexpectedly he spoke in English.

"Ha, you wake? Why you come here, eh?"

Kane asked the inevitable question: "You speak my language—how is that?"

The native grinned.

"I slave—long time, me boy. Me, N'Longa, ju-ju man, me, great fetish. No man like me! You—you hunt brother?"

Kane snarled. "I! Brother! I seek a man, yes."

The native nodded. "Maybe so you find um, eh?"

"He dies!"

Again the native grinned. "Me pow'rful ju-ju man," he announced apropos of nothing. He bent closer. "White man you hunt, eyes like a leopard, eh? Yes? Ha! ha! ha! ha! Listen: man-with-eyes-of-a-leopard, he and Chief Songa make pow'rful palaver; they blood brothers now. Say nothing, I help you; you help me, eh?"

"Why should you help me?" asked Kane suspiciously.

The ju-ju man bent closer and whispered, "White man Songa's right-hand man; Songa more pow'rful than N'Longa. White man mighty ju-ju! N'Longa's white brother kill man-with-eyes-of-a-leopard, be blood brother to N'Longa. N'Longa be more pow'rful than Songa; palaver set."

And like a dusky ghost he floated out of the hut so swiftly that Kane was not sure but that the whole affair was a dream.

Without, Kane could see the flare of fires. The drums were still booming, but close at hand the tones merged and mingled, and the impulse-producing vibrations were lost. All seemed a barbaric clamor without rime or reason, yet there was an undertone of mockery there, savage and gloating.

"Lies," thought Kane, his mind still swimming, "jungle lies like jungle women that lure a man to his doom."

Two warriors entered the hut—savage giants, hideous with paint and armed with crude spears. They lifted the Englishman and carried him out of the hut. They bore him across an open space, leaned him upright against a post and bound him there. About him, behind him and to the side, a great semicircle of dark faces leered and faded in the firelight as the flames leaped and sank. There in front of him loomed a shape hideous and obscene—a black, formless thing, a grotesque parody of a human. Still, brooding, bloodstained, like the formless soul of Africa, the horror, the Black God.

And in front and to each side, upon roughly carven thrones of teakwood, sat two men. He who sat upon the right was a native; huge, ungainly, a gigantic and unlovely mass of flesh and muscles. Small, hog-like eyes blinked out over sin-marked cheeks; huge, flabby red lips pursed in fleshy haughtiness.

The other—

"Ah, Monsieur, we meet again." The speaker was far from being the debonair villain who had taunted Kane in the cavern among the mountains. His clothes were rags; there were more lines in his face; he had sunk lower in the years that had passed. Yet his eyes still gleamed and danced with their old recklessness, and his voice held the same mocking timbre.

"The last time I heard that accursed voice," said Kane calmly, "was in a cave, in darkness, whence you fled like a hunted rat."

"Aye, under different conditions," answered Le Loup imperturbably. "What did you do after blundering about like an elephant in the dark!"

Kane hesitated, then: "I left the mountain—"

"By the front entrance? Yes? I might have known you were too stupid to find the secret door. Hoofs of the Devil, had you thrust against the chest with the golden lock, which stood against the wall, the door had opened to you and revealed the secret passageway through which I went."

"I traced you to the nearest port and there took ship and followed you to Italy, where I found you had gone," said Kane.

"Aye, by the saints, you nearly cornered me in Florence. Ho! ho! ho! I was climbing through a back window while Monsieur Galahad was battering down the front door of the tavern. And had your horse not gone lame, you would have caught up with me on the road to Rome.

"Again, the ship on which I left Spain had barely put out to sea when Monsieur Galahad rides up to the wharfs. Why have you followed me like this? I do not understand."

"Because you are a rogue whom it is my destiny to kill," answered Kane coldly. He did not understand. All his life he had roamed about the world aiding the weak and fighting oppression; he neither knew nor questioned why. That was his obsession, his driving force of life. Cruelty and tyranny to the weak sent a red blaze of fury, fierce and lasting, through his soul. When the full flame of his hatred was wakened and loosed, there was no rest for him until his vengeance had been fulfilled to the uttermost. If he thought of it at all, he considered himself a fulfiller of God's judgment, a vessel of wrath to be emptied upon the souls of the unrighteous. Yet in the full sense of the word Solomon Kane was not wholly a Puritan, though he thought of himself as such.

Le Loup shrugged his shoulders. "I could understand had I wronged you personally. Mon Dieu! I, too, would follow an enemy across the world, but, though I would have joyfully slain and robbed you, I never heard of you until you declared war on me."

Kane was silent, his still fury overcoming him. Though he did not realize it, the Wolf was more than merely an enemy to him; the bandit symbolized to Kane all the things against which the Puritan had fought all his life: cruelty, outrage, oppression and tyranny.

Le Loup broke in on his vengeful meditations. "What did you do with the treasure, which—gods of Hades!—took me years to accumulate? Devil take it, I had time only to snatch a handful of coins and trinkets as I ran."

"I took such as I needed to hunt you down. The rest I gave to the villages which you had looted."

"Saints and the devil!" swore Le Loup. "Monsieur, you are the greatest fool I have yet met. To throw that vast treasure—by Satan, I rage to think of it in the hands of base peasants, vile villagers! Yet, ho! ho! ho! ho! they will steal and kill each other for it. That is human nature."

"Yes, damn you!" flamed Kane suddenly, showing that his conscience had not been at rest. "Doubtless they will, being fools. Yet what could I do? Had I left it there, people might have starved and gone naked for lack of it. More, it would have been found, and theft and slaughter would have followed anyway. You are to blame, for had this treasure been left with its rightful owners, no such trouble would have ensued."

The Wolf grinned without reply. Kane not being a profane man, his rare curses had double effect and always startled his hearers, no matter how vicious or hardened they might be.

It was Kane who spoke next. "Why have you fled from me across the world? You do not really fear me."

"No, you are right. Really I do not know; perhaps flight is a habit which is difficult to break. I made my mistake when I did not kill you that night in the mountains. I am sure I could kill you in a fair fight, yet I have never even, ere now, sought to ambush you. Somehow I have not had a liking to meet you, Monsieur—a whim of mine, a mere whim. Then— mon Dieu!—mayhap I have enjoyed a new sensation —and I had thought that I had exhausted the thrills of life. And then, a man must either be the hunter or the hunted. Until now, Monsieur, I was the hunted, but I grew weary of the role—I thought I had thrown you off the trail."

"A slave, brought from this vicinity, told a Portuguese ship captain of an Englishman who landed from a Spanish ship and went into the jungle. I heard of it and hired the ship, paying the captain to bring me here."

"Monsieur, I admire you for your attempt, but you must admire me, too! Alone I came into this village, and alone among savages and cannibals I—with some slight knowledge of the language learned from a slave aboard ship—I gained the confidence of King Songa and supplanted that mummer, N'Longa. I am a braver man than you, Monsieur, for I had no ship to retreat to, and a ship is waiting for you."

"I admire your courage," said Kane, "but you are content to rule amongst cannibals—you the evilest soul of them all. I intend to return to my own people when I have slain you."

"Your confidence would be admirable were it not amusing. Ho, Gulka!"

A giant savage stalked into the space between them. He was the hugest man that Kane had ever seen, though he moved with cat-like ease and suppleness. His arms and legs were like trees, and the great, sinuous muscles rippled with each motion. His ape-like head was set squarely between gigantic shoulders.

His great, dusky hands were like the talons of an ape, and his brow slanted back from above bestial eyes. Flat nose and great, thick red lips completed this picture of primitive, lustful savagery.

"That is Gulka, the gorilla-slayer," said Le Loup. "He it was who lay in wait beside the trail and smote you down. You are like a wolf, yourself, Monsieur Kane, but since your ship hove in sight you have been watched by many eyes, and had you had all the powers of a leopard, you had not seen Gulka nor heard him. He hunts the most terrible and crafty of all beasts, in their native forests, far to the north, the beasts-who-walk-like-men—as that one, whom he slew some days since."

Kane, following Le Loup's fingers, made out a curious, man-like thing, dangling from a roof-pole of a hut. A jagged end thrust through the thing's body held it there. Kane could scarcely distinguish its characteristics by the firelight, but there was a weird, humanlike semblance about the hideous, hairy thing.

"A female gorilla that Gulka slew and brought to the village," said Le Loup.

The giant slouched close to Kane and stared into the Englishman's eyes. Kane returned his gaze somberly, and presently the savage's eyes dropped sullenly and he slouched back a few paces. The look in the Puritan's grim eyes had pierced the primitive hazes of the gorilla-slayer's soul, and for the first time in his life he felt fear. To throw this off, he tossed a challenging look about; then with unexpected animalness, he struck his huge chest resoundingly, grinned cavernously and flexed his mighty arms. No one spoke. Primordial bestiality had the stage, and the more highly developed types looked on with various feelings of amusement, tolerance or contempt.

Gulka glanced furtively at Kane to see if the Englishman was watching him, then with a sudden beastly roar, plunged forward and dragged a man from the semicircle. While the trembling victim screeched for mercy, the giant hurled him upon the

crude altar before the shadowy idol. A spear rose and
flashed, and the screeching ceased. The Black God
looked on, his monstrous features seeming to leer in
the flickering firelight. He had drunk; was the Black
God pleased with the draft—with the sacrifice?

Gulka stalked back, and stopping before Kane,
flourished the bloody spear before the white man's
face.

Le Loup laughed. Then suddenly N'Longa appeared. He came from nowhere in particular; suddenly he was standing there, beside the post to which
Kane was bound. A lifetime of study of the art of
illusion had given the ju-ju man a highly technical
knowledge of appearing and disappearing—which
after all, consisted only in timing the audience's attention.

He waved Gulka aside with a grand gesture, and
the gorilla-man slunk back, apparently to get out of
N'Longa's gaze—then with incredible swiftness he
turned and struck the ju-ju man a terrific blow upon
the side of the head with his open hand. N'Longa
went down like a felled ox, and in an instant he had
been seized and bound to a post close to Kane. An
uncertain murmuring rose from the tribesmen, which
died out as King Songa stared angrily toward them.

Le Loup leaned back upon his throne and laughed
uproariously.

"The trail ends here, Monsieur Galahad. That ancient fool thought I did not know of his plotting! I was
hiding outside the hut and heard the interesting con-
versation you two had. Ha! ha! ha! ha! The Black God
must drink, Monsieur, but I have persuaded Songa to
have you two burnt; that will be much more enjoyable,
though we shall have to forego the usual feast, I fear.
For after the fires are lit about your feet the devil
himself could not keep your carcasses from becoming
charred frames of bone."

Songa shouted something imperiously, and tribesmen came bearing wood, which they piled about the
feet of N'Longa and Kane. The ju-ju man had re-

covered consciousness, and he now shouted something in his native language. Again the murmuring arose among the shadowy throng. Songa snarled something in reply.

Kane gazed at the scene almost impersonally. Again, somewhere in his soul, dim primal deeps were stirring, age-old thought memories, veiled in the fogs of lost eons. He had been here before, thought Kane; he knew all this of old—the lurid flames beating back the sullen night, the bestial faces leering expectantly, and the god, the Black God, there in the shadows! Always the Black God, brooding back in the shadows. He had known the shouts, the frenzied chant of the worshipers, back there in the gray dawn of the world, the speech of the bellowing drums, the singing priests, the repellent, inflaming, all-pervading scent of freshly spilt blood. All this have I known, somewhere, sometime, thought Kane; now I am the main actor—

He became aware that someone was speaking to him through the roar of the drums; he had not realized that the drums had begun to boom again. The speaker was N'Longa:

"Me pow'rful ju-ju man! Watch now: I work mighty magic. Songa!" His voice rose in a screech that drowned out the wildly clamoring drums.

Songa grinned at the words N'Longa screamed at him. The chant of the drums now had dropped to a low, sinister monotone and Kane plainly heard Le Loup when he spoke:

"N'Longa says that he will now work that magic which it is death to speak, even. Never before has it been worked in the sight of living men; it is the nameless ju-ju magic. Watch closely, Monsieur; possibly we shall be further amused." The Wolf laughed lightly and sardonically.

A savage stooped, applying a torch to the wood about Kane's feet. Tiny jets of flame began to leap up and catch. Another bent to do the same with N'Longa, then hesitated. The ju-ju man sagged in his bonds; his head drooped upon his chest. He seemed dying.

Le Loup leaned forward, cursing: "Feet of the Devil! Is the scoundrel about to cheat us of our pleasure of seeing him writhe in the flames?"

The warrior gingerly touched the wizard and said something in his own language.

Le Loup laughed: "He died of fright. A great wizard, by the—"

His voice trailed off suddenly. The drums stopped as if the drummers had fallen dead simultaneously. Silence dropped like a fog upon the village and in the stillness Kane heard only the sharp crackle of the flames whose heat he was beginning to feel.

All eyes were turned upon the dead man upon the altar, for the corpse had begun to move!

First a twitching of a hand, then an aimless motion of an arm, a motion which gradually spread over the body and limbs. Slowly, with blind, uncertain gestures, the dead man turned upon his side, the trailing limbs found the earth. Then, horribly like something being born, like some frightful reptilian thing bursting the shell of nonexistence, the corpse tottered and reared upright, standing on legs wide apart and stiffly braced, arms still making useless, infantile motions. Utter silence, save somewhere a man's quick breath sounded loud in the stillness.

Kane stared, for the first time in his life smitten speechless and thoughtless. To his Puritan mind this was Satan's hand manifested.

Le Loup sat on his throne, eyes wide and staring, hand still half raised in the careless gesture he was making when frozen into silence by the unbelievable sight. Songa sat beside him, mouth and eyes wide open, fingers making curious jerky motions upon the carved arms of the throne.

Now the corpse was upright, swaying on stilt-like legs, body tilting far back until the sightless eyes seemed to stare straight into the red moon that was just rising over the black jungle. The thing tottered uncertainly in a wide, erratic half-circle, arms flung out grotesquely as if in balance, then swayed about to face the two thrones—and the Black God. A burning twig at Kane's feet cracked like the crash of a cannon in the tense silence. The horror thrust forth a foot—it took a wavering step—another. Then with stiff, jerky and automatonlike steps, legs straddled far apart, the dead man came toward the two who sat in speechless horror to each side of the Black God.

"Ah-h-h!" from somewhere came the explosive sigh, from that shadowy semicircle where crouched the terror-fascinated worshipers. Straight on stalked the grim spector. Now it was within three strides of the thrones, and Le Loup, faced by fear for the first time in his bloody life, cringed back in his chair; while Songa, with a superhuman effort breaking the chains of horror that held him helpless, shattered the night with a wild scream and, springing to his feet, lifted a spear, shrieking and gibbering in wild menace. Then as the ghastly thing halted not its frightful advance, he hurled the spear with all the power of his muscles, and the spear tore through the dead man's breast with a rending of flesh and bone. Not an instant halted the thing—for the dead die not—and Songa the king stood frozen, arms outstretched as if to fend off the terror.

An instant they stood so, leaping firelight and eery moonlight etching the scene forever in the minds of the beholders. The changeless staring eyes of the corpse looked full into the bulging eyes of Songa, where were reflected all the hells of horror.

Then, with a jerky motion, the arms of the thing went out and up. The dead hands fell on Songa's shoulders. At the first touch, the king seemed to shrink and shrivel, and with a scream that was to haunt the dreams of every watcher through all the rest of time, Songa crumpled and fell, and the dead man reeled stiffly and fell with him. Motionless lay the two at the feet of the Black God, and to Kane's dazed mind it seemed that the idol's great, inhuman eyes were fixed upon them with terrible, still laughter.

At the instant of the king's fall, a great shout went

up from the natives, and Kane, with a clarity lent his
subconscious mind by the depths of his hate, looked
for Le Loup and saw him spring from his throne and
vanish in the darkness. Then vision was blurred by a
rush of figures who swept into the space before the
god. Feet knocked aside the blazing brands whose
heat Kane had forgotten, and quick hands freed him;
others loosed the wizard's body and laid it upon the
earth.

Kane dimly understood that the tribesmen believed
this thing to be the work of N'Longa, and that they
connected the vengeance of the wizard with himself.
He bent, laid a hand on the ju-ju man's shoulder. No
doubt of it: he was dead, the flesh was already cold.
He glanced at the other corpses. Songa was dead, too,
and the thing that had slain him lay now without
movement.

Kane started to rise, then halted. Was he dreaming,
or did he really feel a sudden warmth in the dead flesh
he touched? Mind reeling, he again bent over the
wizard's body, and slowly he felt warmness steal over
the limbs and the blood begin to flow sluggishly
through the veins again.

Then N'Longa opened his eyes and stared up into
Kane's, with the blank expression of a newborn babe.
Kane watched, flesh crawling, and saw the knowing,
reptilian glitter come back, saw the wizard's thick lips
part in a wide grin. N'Longa sat up, and a strange
chant arose from the tribesmen.

Kane looked about. The warriors were all kneeling,
swaying their bodies to and fro, and in their shouts
Kane caught the word, "N'Longa!" repeated over and
over in a kind of fearsomely ecstatic refrain of terror
and worship. As the wizard rose, they all fell prostrate.

N'Longa nodded, as if in satisfaction.

"Great ju-ju—great fetish, me!" he announced to
Kane. "You see? My ghost go out—kill Songa—come
back to me! Great magic! Great fetish, me!"

Kane glanced at the Black God looming back in

the shadows, at N'Longa, who now flung out his arms toward the idol as if in invocation.

I am everlasting (Kane thought the Black God said); I drink, no matter who rules; chiefs, slayers, wizards, they pass like the ghosts of dead men through the gray jungle; I stand, I rule; I am the soul of the jungle (said the Black God).

Suddenly Kane came back from the illusory mists in which he had been wandering. "Le Loup! Which way did he flee?"

N'Longa shouted something. A score of hands pointed; from somewhere Kane's rapier was thrust out to him. The fogs faded and vanished; again he was the avenger, the scourge of the unrighteous; with the sudden volcanic speed of a tiger he snatched the sword and was gone.

CHAPTER 5

THE END OF THE TRAIL

Limbs and vines slapped against Kane's face. The oppressive steam of the tropic night rose like mist about him. The moon, now floating high above the jungle, limned the black shadows in its white glow and patterned the jungle floor in grotesque designs. Kane knew not if the man he sought was ahead of him, but broken limbs and trampled underbrush showed that some man had gone that way, some man who fled in haste; nor halted to pick his way.

Kane followed these signs unswervingly. Believing in the justice of his vengeance, he did not doubt that the dim beings who rule men's destinies would finally bring him face to face with Le Loup.

Behind him the drums boomed and muttered. What a tale they had to tell this night! of the triumph of N'Longa, the death of Songa the King, the overthrow of the man-with-eyes-like-a-leopard, and a more dark-

some tale, a tale to be whispered in low, muttering
vibrations: the nameless ju-ju.

Was he dreaming? Kane wondered as he hurried
on. Was all this part of some foul magic? He had seen
a dead man rise and slay and die again; he had seen
a man die and come to life again. Did N'Longa in
truth send his ghost, his soul, his life essence forth
into the void, dominating a corpse to do his will?
Aye, N'Longa died a real death there, bound to the
torture stake, and he who lay dead on the altar rose
and did as N'Longa would have done had he been
free. Then, the unseen force animating the dead man
fading, N'Longa had lived again.

Yes, Kane thought, he must admit it as a fact.
Somewhere in the darksome reaches of jungle and
river, N'Longa had stumbled upon the Secret—the
Secret of controlling life and death, of overcoming the
shackles and limitations of the flesh. How had this
dark wisdom, born in the black and blood-stained
shadows of this grim land, been given to the wizard?
What sacrifice had been so pleasing to the Black Gods,
what ritual so monstrous, as to make them give up the
knowledge of this magic? And what thoughtless, time-
less journeys had N'Longa taken, when he chose to
send his ego, his ghost, through the far, misty countries, reached only by death?

There is wisdom in the shadows (brooded the
drums), wisdom and magic; go into the darkness for
wisdom; ancient magic shuns the light; we remember
the lost ages (whispered the drums), ere man became
wise and foolish; we remember the beast gods—the
serpent gods and the ape gods and the nameless, the
Black Gods, they who drank blood and whose voices
roared through the shadowy hills, who feasted and
lusted. The secrets of life and of death are theirs; we
remember, we remember (sang the drums).

Kane heard them as he hastened on. The tale they
told to the feathered warriors farther up the river, he
could translate; but they spoke to him in their own
way, and that language was deeper, more basic.

The moon, high in the dark blue skies, lighted his way and gave him a clear vision as he came out at last into a glade and saw Le Loup standing there. The Wolf's naked blade was a long gleam of silver in the moon, and he stood with shoulders thrown back, the old, defiant smile still on his face.

"A long trail, Monsieur," said he. "It began in the mountains of France; it ends in an African jungle. I have wearied of the game at last, Monsieur—and you die. I had not fled from the village, even, save that—I admit it freely—that damnable witchcraft of N'Longa's shook my nerves. More, I saw that the whole tribe would turn against me."

Kane advanced warily, wondering what dim, forgotten tinge of chivalry in the bandit's soul had caused him thus to take his chance in the open. He half suspected treachery, but his keen eyes could detect no shadow of movement in the jungle on either side of the glade.

"Monsieur, on guard!" Le Loup's voice was crisp. "Time that we ended this fool's dance about the world. Here we are alone."

The men were now within reach of each other, and Le Loup, in the midst of his sentence, suddenly plunged forward with the speed of light, thrusting viciously. A slower man had died there, but Kane parried and sent his own blade in a silver streak that slit Le Loup's tunic as the Wolf bounded backward. Le Loup admitted the failure of his trick with a wild laugh and came in with the breath-taking speed and fury of a tiger, his blade making a white fan of steel about him.

Rapier clashed on rapier as the two swordsmen fought. They were fire and ice opposed. Le Loup fought wildly but craftily, leaving no openings, taking advantage of every opportunity. He was a living flame, bounding back, leaping in, feinting, thrusting, warding, striking—laughing like a wild man, taunting and cursing.

Kane's skill was cold, calculating, scintillant. He made no waste movement, no motion not absolutely necessary. He seemed to devote more time and effort toward defense than did Le Loup, yet there was no hesitancy in his attack, and when he thrust, his blade shot out with the speed of a striking snake.

There was little to choose between the men as to height, strength and reach. Le Loup was the swifter by a scant, flashing margin, but Kane's skill reached a finer point of perfection. The Wolf's fencing was fiery, dynamic, like the blast from a furnace. Kane was more steady—less the instinctive, more the thinking fighter, though he, too, was a born slayer, with the co-ordination that only a natural fighter possessed.

Thrust, parry, a feint, a sudden whirl of blades—

"Ha!" the Wolf sent up a shout of ferocious laughter as the blood started from a cut on Kane's cheek. As if the sight drove him to further fury, he attacked like the beast men named him. Kane was forced back before that blood-lusting onslaught, but the Puritan's expression did not alter.

Minutes flew by; the clang and clash of steel did not diminish. Now they stood squarely in the center of the glade, Le Loup untouched, Kane's garments red with the blood that oozed from wounds on cheek, breast, arm and thigh. The Wolf grinned savagely and mockingly in the moonlight, but he had begun to doubt.

His breath came hissing fast and his arm began to weary; who was this man of steel and ice who never seemed to weaken? Le Loup knew that the wounds he had inflicted on Kane were not deep, but even so, the steady flow of blood should have sapped some of the man's strength and speed by this time. But if Kane felt the ebb of his powers, it did not show. His brooding countenance did not change in expression, and he pressed the fight with as much cold fury as at the beginning.

Le Loup felt his might fading, and with one last

desperate effort he rallied all his fury and strength
into a single plunge. A sudden, unexpected attack too
wild and swift for the eye to follow, a dynamic burst
of speed and fury no man could have withstood, and
Solomon Kane reeled for the first time as he felt cold
steel tear through his body. He reeled back, and Le
Loup with a wild shout, plunged after him, his red-
dened sword free, a gasping taunt on his lips.

Kane's sword, backed by the force of desperation,
met Le Loup's in midair; met, held and wrenched.
The Wolf's yell of triumph died on his lips as his
sword flew singing from his hand.

For a fleeting instant he stopped short, arms flung
wide as a crucifix, and Kane heard his wild, mocking
laughter peal forth for the last time, as the Englishman's rapier made a silver line in the moonlight.

Far away came the mutter of the drums. Kane
mechanically cleansed his sword on his tattered garments. The trail ended here, and Kane was conscious
of a strange feeling of futility. He always felt that,
after he had killed a foe. Somehow it always seemed
that no real good had been wrought; as if the foe had,
after all, escaped his just vengeance.

With a shrug of his shoulders Kane turned his attention to his bodily needs. Now that the heat of battle
had passed, he began to feel weak and faint from the
loss of blood. That last thrust had been close; had he
not managed to avoid its full point by a twist of his
body, the blade had transfixed him. As it was, the
sword had struck glancingly, plowed along his ribs
and sunk deep in the muscles beneath the shoulder-
blade, inflicting a long and shallow wound.

Kane looked about him and saw that a small stream
trickled through the glade at the far side. Here he
made the only mistake of that kind that he ever made
in his entire life. Mayhap he was dizzy from loss of
blood and still mazed from the weird happenings of
the night; be that as it may, he laid down his rapier

and crossed, weaponless, to the stream. There he laved
his wounds and bandaged them as best he could, with
strips torn from his clothing.

Then he rose and was about to retrace his steps
when a motion among the trees on the side of the
glade where he first entered, caught his eye. A huge
figure stepped out of the jungle, and Kane saw, and
recognized, his doom. The man was Gulka, the gorilla-
slayer. Kane remembered that he had not seen the
giant among those doing homage to N'Longa. How
could he know the craft and hatred in that slanting
skull that had led the savage fighter, escaping the
vengeance of his tribesmen, to trail down the only
man he had ever feared?

The Black God had been kind to his neophyte; had
led him upon his victim helpless and unarmed. Now
Gulka could kill his man openly—and slowly, as a
leopard kills, not smiting him down from ambush as
he had planned, silently and suddenly.

A wide grin split the giant's face, and he moistened
his lips. Kane, watching him, was coldly and deliberately weighing his chances. Gulka had already spied
the rapiers. He was closer to them than was Kane.
The Englishman knew that there was no chance of his
winning in a sudden race for the swords.

A slow, deadly rage surged in him—the fury of
helplessness. The blood churned in his temples and
his eyes smoldered with a terrible light as he eyed the
warrior. His fingers spread and closed like claws. They
were strong, those hands; men had died in their clutch.
Even Gulka's huge column of a neck might break like
a rotten branch between them—a wave of weakness
made the futility of these thoughts apparent to an
extent that needed not the verification of the moonlight glimmering from the spear in Gulka's hand. Kane
could not even have fled had he wished—and he had
never fled from a single foe.

The gorilla-slayer moved out into the glade. Massive, terrible, he was the personification of the primitive, the Stone Age. His mouth yawned in a red cavern

of a grin; he bore himself with the haughty arrogance of savage might.

Kane tensed himself for the struggle that could end but one way. He strove to rally his waning forces. Useless; he had lost too much blood. At least he would meet his death on his feet, and somehow he stiffened his buckling knees and held himself erect, though the glade shimmered before him in uncertain waves and the moonlight seemed to have become a red fog through which he dimly glimpsed the approaching man.

Kane stooped, though the effort nearly pitched him on his face; he dipped water in his cupped hands and dashed it into his face. This revived him, and he straightened, hoping that Gulka would charge and get it over with before his weakness crumpled him to the earth.

Gulka was now about the center of the glade, moving with the slow, easy stride of a great cat stalking a victim. He was not at all in a hurry to consummate his purpose. He wanted to toy with his victim, to see fear come into those grim eyes which had looked him down, even when the possessor of those eyes had been bound to the death stake. He wanted to slay, at last, slowly, glutting his tigerish blood-lust and torture-lust to the fullest extent.

Then suddenly he halted, turned swiftly, facing another side of the glade. Kane, wondering, followed his glance.

At first it seemed like a blacker shadow among the jungle shadows. At first there was no motion, no sound, but Kane instinctively knew that some terrible menace lurked there in the darkness that masked and merged the silent trees. A sullen horror brooded there, and Kane felt as if, from that monstrous shadow, inhuman eyes seared his very soul. Yet simultaneously there came the fantastic sensation that these eyes were not directed on him. He looked at the gorilla-slayer. The giant had apparently forgotten him; he stood, half crouching, spear lifted, eyes fixed upon that clump of blackness. Kane looked again. Now there was motion in the shadows; they merged fantastically and moved out into the glade, much as Gulka had done. Kane blinked: was this the illusion that precedes death? The shape he looked upon was such as he had visioned dimly in wild nightmares, when the wings of sleep bore him back through lost ages.

He thought at first it was some blasphemous mockery of a man, for it went erect and was tall as a tall man. But it was inhumanly broad and thick, and its gigantic arms hung nearly to its misshapen feet.

Then the moonlight smote full upon its bestial face, and Kane's mazed mind thought that the thing was the Black God coming out of the shadows, animated and blood-lusting. Then he saw that it was covered with hair, and he remembered the man-like thing dangling from the roof-pole in the native village. He looked at Gulka.

The warrior was facing the gorilla, spear at the charge. He was not afraid, but his sluggish mind was wondering over the miracle that brought this beast so far from his native jungles.

The mighty ape came out into the moonlight and there was a terrible majesty about his movements. He was nearer Kane than Gulka but he did not seem to be aware of the Puritan. His small, blazing eyes were fixed on the giant native with terrible intensity. He advanced with a curious swaying stride.

Far away the drums whispered through the night, like an accompaniment to this grim Stone Age drama. The savage crouched in the middle of the glade, but the primordial came out of the jungle with eyes blood-shot and blood-lusting. The warrior was face to face with a thing more primitive than he. Again ghosts of memories whispered to Kane: you have seen such sights before (they murmured), back in the dim days, the dawn days, when beast and beast-man battled for supremacy.

Gulka moved away from the ape in a half-circle, crouching, spear ready. With all his craft he was seeking to trick the gorilla, to make a swift kill, for he had never before met such a monster as this, and though he did not fear, he had begun to doubt. The ape made no attempt to stalk or circle; he strode straight forward toward Gulka.

The powerful warrior who faced him and the Englishman who watched could not know the brutish love, the brutish hate that had driven the monster down from the low, forest-covered hills of the north to follow for leagues the trail of him who was the scourge of his kind—the slayer of his mate, whose body now hung from the roof-pole of the native village.

The end came swiftly, almost like a sudden gesture. They were close, now, beast and beast-man; and suddenly, with an earth-shaking roar, the gorilla charged. A great hairy arm smote aside the thrusting spear, and the ape closed with the warrior. There was a shattering sound as of many branches breaking simultaneously, and Gulka slumped silently to the earth, to lie with arms, legs and body flung in strange, unnatural positions. The ape towered an instant above him, like a statue of the primordial triumphant.

Far away Kane heard the drums murmur. The soul of the jungle, the soul of the jungle: this phrase surged through his mind with monotonous reiteration.

The three who had stood in power before the Black God that night, where were they? Back in the village where the drums rustled lay Songa—King Songa, once lord of life and death, now a shriveled corpse with a face set in a mask of horror. Stretched on his back in the middle of the glade lay he whom Kane had followed many a league by land and sea. And Gulka the gorilla-slayer lay at the feet of his killer, broken at last by the savagery which had made him a true son of this grim land which had at last overwhelmed him.

Yet the Black God still reigned, thought Kane

dizzily, brooding back in the shadows of this dark country, bestial, blood-lusting, caring naught who lived or died, so that he drank.

Kane watched the mighty ape, wondering how long it would be before the huge simian spied and charged him. But the gorilla gave no evidence of having ever seen him. Some dim impulse of vengeance yet unglutted prompting him, he bent and raised the warrior. Then he slouched toward the jungle, Gulka's limbs trailing limply and grotesquely. As he reached the trees, the ape halted, whirling the giant form high in the air with seemingly no effort, and dashed the dead man up among the branches. There was a rending sound as a broken projecting limb tore through the body hurled so powerfully against it, and the dead gorilla-slayer dangled there hideously.

A moment the clear moon limned the great ape in its glimmer, as he stood silently gazing up at his victim; then like a dark shadow he melted noiselessly into the jungle.

Kane walked slowly to the middle of the glade and took up his rapier. The blood had ceased to flow from his wounds, and some of his strength was returning, enough, at least, for him to reach the coast where his ship awaited him. He halted at the edge of the glade for a backward glance at Le Loup's upturned face and still form, white in the moonlight, and at the dark shadow among the trees that was Gulka, left by some bestial whim, hanging as the she-gorilla hung in the village.

Afar the drums muttered: "The wisdom of our land is ancient; the wisdom of our land is dark; whom we serve, we destroy. Flee if you would live, but you will never forget our chant. Never, never," sang the drums.

Kane turned to the trail which led to the beach and the ship waiting there.

RATTLE OF BONES

"Landlord, ho!" The shout broke the lowering silence and reverberated through the black forest with sinister echoing.

"This place hath a forbidding aspect, meseemeth."

Two men stood in front of the forest tavern. The building was low, long and rambling, built of heavy logs. Its small windows were heavily barred and the door was closed. Above the door its sinister sign showed faintly—a cleft skull.

This door swung slowly open and a bearded face peered out. The owner of the face stepped back and motioned his guests to enter—with a grudging gesture it seemed. A candle gleamed on a table; a flame smoldered in the fireplace.

"Your names?"

"Solomon Kane," said the taller man briefly.

"Gaston l'Armon," the other spoke curtly. "But what is that to you?"

"Strangers are few in the Black Forest," grunted the host, "bandits many. Sit at yonder table and I will bring food."

The two men sat down, with the bearing of men who have traveled far. One was a tall gaunt man, clad in a featherless hat and somber black garments, which set off the dark pallor of his forbidding face. The other was of a different type entirely, bedecked with lace and plumes, although his finery was somewhat stained from travel. He was handsome in a bold way, and his restless eyes shifted from side to side, never still an instant.

53

The host brought wine and food to the rough-hewn table and then stood back in the shadows, like a somber image. His features, now receding into vagueness, now luridly etched in the firelight as it leaped and flickered, were masked in a beard which seemed almost animal-like in thickness. A great nose curved above this beard and two small red eyes stared unblinkingly at his guests.

"Who are you?" suddenly asked the younger man.

"I am the host of the Cleft Skull Tavern," sullenly replied the other. His tone seemed to challenge his questioner to ask further.

"Do you have many guests?" l'Armon pursued.

"Few come twice," the host grunted.

Kane started and glanced up straight into those small red eyes, as if he sought for some hidden meaning in the host's words. The flaming eyes seemed to dilate, then dropped sullenly before the Englishman's cold stare.

"I'm for bed," said Kane abruptly, bringing his meal to a close. "I must take up my journey by daylight."

"And I," added the Frenchman. "Host, show us to our chambers."

Black shadows wavered on the walls as the two followed their silent host down a long, dark hall. The stocky, broad body of their guide seemed to grow and expand in the light of the small candle which he carried, throwing a long, grim shadow behind him.

At a certain door he halted, indicating that they were to sleep there. They entered; the host lit a candle with the one he carried, then lurched back the way he had come.

In the chamber the two men glanced at each other. The only furnishings of the room were a couple of bunks, a chair or two and a heavy table.

"Let us see if there be any way to make fast the door," said Kane. "I like not the looks of mine host."

"There are racks on the door and jamb for a bar," said Gaston, "but no bar."

"We might break up the table and use its pieces for a bar," mused Kane.

"Mon Dieu," said l'Armon, "you are timorous, m'sieu."

Kane scowled. "I like not being murdered in my sleep," he answered gruffly.

"My faith!" the Frenchman laughed. "We are chance met—until I overtook you on the forest road an hour before sunset, we had never seen each other."

"I have seen you somewhere before," answered Kane, "though I can not now recall where. As for the other, I assume every man is an honest fellow until he shows me he is a rogue; moreover I am a light sleeper and slumber with a pistol at hand."

The Frenchman laughed again.

"I was wondering how m'sieu could bring himself to sleep in the room with a stranger! Ha! Ha! All right, m'sieu Englishman, let us go forth and take a bar from one of the other rooms."

Taking the candle with them, they went into the corridor. Utter silence reigned and the small candle twinkled redly and evilly in the thick darkness.

"Mine host hath neither guests nor servants," muttered Solomon Kane. "A strange tavern. What is the name, now? These German words come not easily to me—the Cleft Skull? A bloody name, i'faith."

They tried the rooms next to theirs, but no bar rewarded their search. Finally, they came to the last room at the end of the corridor. They entered. It was furnished like the rest, except that the door was provided with a small barrel opening, and fastened from the outside with a heavy bolt which was secured at one end to the door-jamb. They raised the bolt and looked in.

"There should be an outer window, but there is not," muttered Kane. "Look!"

The floor was stained darkly. The walls and the one bunk were hacked in places, great splinters having been torn away.

"Men have died in here," said Kane, somberly. "Is yonder not a bar fixed in the wall?"

"Aye, but 'tis made fast," said the Frenchman, tugging at it. "The—"

A section of the wall swung back and Gaston gave a quick exclamation. A small, secret room was revealed, and the two men bent over the grisly thing that lay upon its floor.

"The skeleton of a man!" said Gaston. "And behold, how his bony leg is shackled to the floor! He was imprisoned here and died."

"Nay," said Kane, "the skull is cleft—methinks mine host had a grim reason for the name of his hellish tavern. This man, like us, was no doubt a wanderer who fell into the fiend's hands."

"Likely," said Gaston without interest; he was engaged in idly working the great iron ring from the skeleton's leg bones. Failing in this, he drew his sword and with an exhibition of remarkable strength cut the chain which joined the ring on the leg to a ring set deep in the log floor.

"Why should he shackle a skeleton to the floor?" mused the Frenchman. "Monbleu! 'Tis a waste of good chain. Now, m'sieu," he ironically addressed the white heap of bones, "I have freed you and you may go where you like!"

"Have done!" Kane's voice was deep. "No good will come of mocking the dead."

"The dead should defend themselves," laughed l'Armon. "Somehow, I will slay the man who kills me, though my corpse climb up forty fathoms of ocean to do it."

Kane turned toward the outer door, closing the door of the secret room behind him. He liked not this talk which smacked of demonry and witchcraft; and he was in haste to face the host with the charge of his guilt.

As he turned, with his back to the Frenchman, he felt the touch of cold steel against his neck and knew that a pistol muzzle was pressed close beneath the base of his brain.

"Move not, m'sieu!" The voice was low and silky. "Move not, or I will scatter your few brains over the room."

The Puritan, raging inwardly, stood with his hands in the air while l'Armon slipped his pistols and sword from their sheaths.

"Now you can turn," said Gaston, stepping back.

Kane bent a grim eye on the dapper fellow, who stood bareheaded now, hat in one hand, the other hand leveling his long pistol.

"Gaston the Butcher!" said the Englishman somberly. "Fool that I was to trust a Frenchman! You range far, murderer! I remember you now, with that cursed great hat off—I saw you in Calais some years agone."

"Aye—and now you will see me never again. What was that?"

"Rats exploring the skeleton," said Kane, watching the bandit like a hawk, waiting for a single slight wavering of the black gun muzzle. "The sound was of the rattle of bones."

"Like enough," returned the other. "Now, M'sieu Kane, I know you carry considerable money on your person. I had thought to wait until you slept and then slay you, but the opportunity presented itself and I took it. You trick easily."

"I had little thought that I should fear a man with whom I had broken bread," said Kane, a deep timbre of slow fury sounding in his voice.

The bandit laughed cynically. His eyes narrowed as he began to back slowly toward the outer door. Kane's sinews tensed involuntarily; he gathered himself like a giant wolf about to launch himself in a death leap, but Gaston's hand was like a rock and the pistol never trembled.

"We will have no death plunges after the shot," said Gaston. "Stand still, m'sieu; I have seen men killed by dying men, and I wish to have distance enough between us to preclude that possibility. My faith—I will shoot, you will roar and charge, but you will die before you reach me with your bare hands. And mine host will have another skeleton in his secret niche. That is, if I do not kill him myself. The fool knows me not, nor I him, moreover—"

The Frenchman was in the doorway now, sighting along the barrel. The candle, which had been stuck in a niche on the wall, shed a weird and flickering light which did not extend past the doorway. And with the suddenness of death, from the darkness behind Gaston's back, a broad, vague form rose up and a gleaming blade swept down. The Frenchman went to his knees like a butchered ox, his brains spilling from his cleft skull. Above him towered the figure of the host, a wild and terrible spectacle, still holding the hanger with which he had slain the bandit.

"Ho! Ho!" he roared. "Back!"

Kane had leaped forward as Gaston fell, but the host thrust into his very face a long pistol which he held in his left hand.

"Back!" he repeated in a tigerish roar, and Kane retreated from the menacing weapon and the insanity in the red eyes.

The Englishman stood silent, his flesh crawling as he sensed a deeper and more hideous threat than the Frenchman had offered. There was something inhuman about this man, who now swayed to and fro like some great forest beast while his mirthless laughter boomed out again.

"Gaston the Butcher!" he shouted, kicking the corpse at his feet. "Ho! Ho! My fine brigand will hunt no more; I had heard of this fool who roamed the Black Forest—he wished gold and he found death! Now your gold shall be mine; and more than gold—vengeance!"

"I am no foe of yours," Kane spoke calmly.

"All men are my foes! Look—the marks on my wrists! See—the marks on my ankles! And deep in my back—the kiss of the knout! And deep in my brain, the wounds of the years of the cold, silent cells where I lay as punishment for a crime I never committed!" The voice broke in a hideous, grotesque sob.

Kane made no answer. This man was not the first he had seen whose brain had shattered amid the horrors of the terrible Continental prisons.

"But I escaped!" the scream rose triumphantly, "and here I make war on all men. . . . What was that?"

Did Kane see a flash of fear in those hideous eyes?

"My sorcerer is rattling his bones!" whispered the host, then laughed wildly. "Dying, he swore his very bones would weave a net of death for me. I shackled his corpse to the floor, and now, deep in the night, I hear his bare skeleton clash and rattle as he seeks to be free, and I laugh! Ho! Ho! How he yearns to rise and stalk like old King Death along these dark corridors when I sleep, to slay me in my bed!"

Suddenly the insane eyes flared hideously: "You were in that secret room, you and this dead fool! Did he talk to you?"

Kane shuddered in spite of himself. Was it insanity or did he actually hear the faint rattle of bones, as if the skeleton had moved slightly? Kane shrugged his shoulders; rats will even tug at dusty bones.

The host was laughing again. He sidled around Kane, keeping the Englishman always covered, and with his free hand opened the door. All was darkness within, so that Kane could not even see the glimmer of the bones on the floor.

"All men are my foes!" mumbled the host, in the incoherent manner of the insane. "Why should I spare any man? Who lifted a hand to my aid when I lay for years in the vile dungeons of Karlsruhe—and for a deed never proven? Something happened to my brain, then. I became as a wolf—a brother to these of the Black Forest to which I fled when I escaped.

"They have feasted, my brothers, on all who lay in my tavern—all except this one who now clashes his bones, this magician from Russia. Lest he come stalking back through the black shadows when night is over the world, and slay me—for who may slay the dead!—I stripped his bones and shackled him. His sorcery was not powerful enough to save him from me, but all men know that a dead magician is more evil than a living one. Move not, Englishman! Your bones I shall leave in this secret room beside this one, to—"

The maniac was standing partly in the doorway of the secret room, now, his weapon still menacing Kane. Suddenly he seemed to topple backward, and vanished in the darkness; and at the same instant a vagrant gust of wind swept the door shut behind him. The candle on the wall flickered and went out. Kane's groping hands, sweeping over the floor, found a pistol, and he straightened, facing the door where the maniac had vanished. He stood in the utter darkness, his blood freezing, while a hideous muffled screaming came from the secret room, intermingled with the dry, grisly rattle of fleshless bones. Then silence fell.

Kane found flint and steel and lighted the candle. Then, holding it in one hand and the pistol in the other, he opened the secret door.

"Great God!" he muttered as cold sweat formed on his body. "This thing is beyond all reason, yet with mine own eyes I see it! Two vows have here been kept, for Gaston the Butcher swore that even in death he would avenge his slaying, and his was the hand which set yon fleshless monster free. And he—"

The host of the Cleft Skull lay lifeless on the floor of the secret room, his bestial face set in lines of terrible fear; and deep in his broken neck were sunk the bare fingerbones of the sorcerer's skeleton.

THE CASTLE OF THE DEVIL

A rider was singing down the forest trail in the growing twilight, keeping time to his horse's easy jog. He was a tall rangy man, broad of shoulder and deep of chest, with keen restless eyes which seemed at once to challenge and mock.

"Hola!" he drew his horse to a sudden stop and looked down curiously at the man who rose from his seat on a stone beside the road. This man was even taller than the rider—a lean somber man clad in plain dark garments, his features a dark pallor.

"An Englishman? And a Puritan by the cut o' that garb," commented the man on the horse. "I am glad to see a countryman in this outlandish domain, even such a melancholy fellow as you seem. My name is John Silent and I am bound for Genoa."

"I am Solomon Kane," the other answered in a deep measured voice. "I am a wanderer on the face of the earth and have no destination."

John Silent frowned down at the Puritan in puzzlement. The deep cold eyes gazed back at him, unswerving.

"Name of the Devil, man, know you not whither you are bound at present?"

"Wherever the spirit moves me to go," answered Kane. "Just now I find myself in this wild and desolate country through which I journey, doubtless drawn hither for some purpose yet unknown to me."

Silent sighed and shook his head.

"Mount behind me, man, and we will at least seek some tavern in which to spend the night."

61

"I would not overtax your steed, good sir, but if you will permit, I will walk along by your side and converse with you, for it is many a month since I have heard good English speech."

As they went slowly down the trail, John Silent still gazed down at the man, noting the stride that was long and cat-like in spite of Kane's lank build, and the long rapier which hung at his hip. Silent's hand instinctively touched the long curved hanger in his own belt.

"Do you mean to tell me that you journey through the countries of the world with no goal in view, caring not where you may be?"

"Sir, what matters it where a man be if he is carrying out God's plan for him?"

"By Jove," swore John Silent, "you are even more wayward than I, for though I rove the world also, I always have some goal in mind. As now I come from the command of a troop of soldiery and am going to Genoa to go on board a ship which sails against the Turkish corsairs. Come with me, friend, and learn to sail the seas."

"I have sailed them and found them to be little to my liking. Many who call themselves honest merchantmen be naught but bloody pirates."

John Silent hid his grin and changed the subject.

"Then, since the spirit has moved you to traverse this land, 'tis like you have found something to your liking herein?"

"No, good sir, I find little here but starving peasants, cruel lords and lawless men. Yet 'tis like that I have done somewhat of good, for only a few hours agone I came upon a wretch who hung on a gallows and cut him down ere his breath had passed from him."

John Silent nearly fell out of his saddle.

"What! You cut down a man from Baron Von Staler's gibbet? Name of the Devil, you will have both our necks in a noose!"

"You should not curse so hotly," Kane reproved

mildly. "I know not this Baron Von Staler, but me-thinks he had hanged a man unjustly. The victim was only a boy and he had a good face."

"And forsooth," said John Silent angrily, "you must risk our lives by saving his worthless one, which was already doomed."

"What else was there to do?" asked Kane with a touch of impatience. "I beg you, vex me no more on the subject but tell me whose castle it is that I see rising above the trees."

"One which you may come to know much more thoroughly if we make not haste," Silent answered grimly. "That is the keep of Baron Von Staler, whose gibbet you robbed, and who is the most powerful lord in the Black Forest. There goes the path which leads up the steep to his door; here is the road we take—the one that leads us quickest and furtherest out of the good Baron's reach."

"Methinks that is the castle which the peasants have spoken to me of," mused Kane. "They call it an un-savory name—the Castle of the Devil. Come, let us look into the matter."

"You mean go up to the castle?" cried Silent, staring.

"Aye, sir. The Baron will scarce refuse two way-farers a lodging. More, we can ascertain what sort of a man he is. I would like to see this lord who hangs children."

"And if you like him not?" asked Silent sarcastically.

Kane sighed. "It has fallen upon me, now and again in my sojourns through the world, to ease various evil men of their lives. I have a feeling that it will prove thus with the Baron."

"Name of two devils!" swore Silent in amazement. "You speak as if you were a judge on a bench and Baron Von Staler bound helpless before you, instead of being as it is—you but one blade and the Baron surrounded by lusty men-at-arms."

"The right is on my side," said Kane somberly. "And right is mightier than a thousand men-at-arms.

But why all this talk? I have not yet seen the Baron, and who am I to pass judgment unseen. Mayhap the Baron is a righteous man."

Silent shook his head in wonder.

"You are either an inspired maniac, a fool, or the most courageous man in the world!" he laughed suddenly. "Lead on! 'Tis a wild venture that's like to end in death, but its insanity appeals to me and no man can say that John Silent fails to follow where another man leads!"

"Your speech is wild and Godless," said Kane, "but I begin to like you."

Kane rode along the track that rose between the fir trees, toward the castle. Silent followed on his horse, its hooves clattering on shards of granite. When it threatened to stumble, he dismounted and led the beast.

The path doubled back constantly. Huge ferns made the depths of the forest seem dismal and primeval. Again and again the Puritan thought they had reached the approach to the castle, but always the building mounted higher above the trees, as though striving to rise above the world. The innumerable firs threshed and groaned softly, like a gathering of mourners. Otherwise the track was heavy with silence, which made their harsh footfalls violent and unnerving.

At last, when even Kane's easy stride was faltering a little, they came in sight of the castle. Their climb had kept pace with the light; here on the granite height it was still not entirely dark. The castle looked one with the rock on which it stood. Granite towers and battlements massed against the gloomily luminous sky.

But Kane was not concerned at that moment with the building. Among the firs beside the track a horse waited silently. Even in the twilight he sensed that there was something wrong with it. Silent made to follow him, but his steed baulked, and he had to tether it to a tree.

"Methinks this castle is aptly named the abode of a devil," Kane muttered furiously, gazing at the still horse. It was long dead, and decayed; chains held it standing. But decay could not account for the fact that it had been crudely blinded.

Silent gripped Kane's arm fiercely in his anger. "By the bones of the saints!" he swore. "What kind of monster wounds a poor beast so?"

His violence distracted Kane momentarily. In that moment Kane knew that they were not alone among the trees. Before he could act, several men surrounded them, silent as ghosts. But the men were solid enough, for their sword-points pricked the Englishmen's throats, while one of the swordsmen disarmed them.

The oldest swordsman confronted them. Like the rest, he was tall as Kane. He wore no armor, but was dressed in gray rather drab clothes. He carried only a sword. Beneath his thick gray hair his broad wizened face looked weathered as the granite. His expression seemed less menacing than sadly resigned. "What business have you on the lands of Baron Von Staler?" he demanded in a deep cracked voice.

"Why," Silent replied before Kane could voice his wrath, "we are Englishmen abroad in the Black Forest. Seeing the Baron's castle from afar, we thought he would not refuse two weary travellers hospitality."

The old man scrutinized his eyes, as if he might be using the twilight to obscure the truth. "Perhaps that is so," he said at last. "You must tell your tale to my master."

The men—a dozen of them, Kane counted—sheathed their swords almost noiselessly, but did not return the Englishmen's weapons. They paced their captives stealthily. "Bring the Englishman's horse," the old man told the youngest, a lithe but broad-shouldered youth. "You need not fear," he told Silent, glimpsing his expression. "No harm will befall your steed."

As they reached the courtyard, Kane saw that the castle was overgrown and, in places, crumbling. It seemed on the edge of ruin, as though relinquishing its shape in order to merge again with the rock. He shivered, not only from the chill of granite that enclosed him. The castle felt to him as though it had lost its soul.

They entered the castle. He observed that the great door was almost soundless. "Please remove your shoes," the old man said.

An Oriental practice, thought Kane. But the man explained "My master requires quiet. Never raise your voice here, for you would be risking your life."

He led the way into dimness. Kane had never seen an inhabited building so dark. On the walls, a few torches struggled with the shadows. The granite smelled damp as a cave. He sensed that the passage was high, but dank blackness hovered lower than the ceiling. Beside him Silent glanced rapidly about, wary as a trapped beast.

At last they emerged into the main hall. There was more light here, for a great log fire blazed in an immense hearth. On the walls, weapons flickered in a parody of combat, bathed in the glow as though in blood. Among them were the heads of many animals. Firelight panted in their mouths and glared from their dead eyes.

Beside the hearth stood a man dressed in black. He was large-boned, and taller than Kane. He turned to the men as they entered, stooping toward them as though burdened like Atlas. He was bald; his face seemed pared down to skin and massive bone. "There are two strangers with you, Kurt," he said, almost whispering.

"Two Englishmen, Herr Baron," the old man said.

"Englishmen." He lingered over the word as though it were a rare delicacy. "And what is your name, Englishman who moves like a great cat?"

He was staring at Kane; flames filled his eyes. Something about him disturbed Kane; he had dignity and quiet power, yet these qualities seemed spoiled, perhaps turned into cruelty. And there was something else — "My name is Solomon Kane," the Puritan said, remembering to restrain his voice.

"You name yourself with pride, as a man should. And what is your name, strider?"

"John Silent," he said, speaking low.

"Indeed! Well, if you are aptly named, you will be welcome here. But what mission— Hark!"

He had frozen, extending one hand to command silence. Kane could hear nothing except the crepitant song of the fire. The men-at-arms were intent as their master, and hardly breathing. "She is calling, Kurt," the Baron said.

The old man hurried away, up a wide staircase in the further reaches of the hall. The Baron straightened up a little; he looked like a leaning tree whose roots were losing their grip on the earth. The men-at-arms relaxed, but remained silently watching the Englishmen.

"You were speaking of your mission here," the Baron said to Kane, as though it had been the Puritan who had interrupted.

"I have but one mission, wherever Providence may choose to take me," Kane said, in a low voice more intense than any shout. "To seek evil and relieve the world of it."

The Baron stared at him, and Kane was sure that there was something odd about his eyes. "I have not heard a man speak so frankly here for years," he said. "You sound to be a man of honor, Englishman. And has your search of my lands been rewarded?"

Silent made a surreptitious gesture to Kane to take care. Without looking at him, the Baron said, "Control yourself, my silent friend. I believe your companion cannot lie."

He had the measure of Kane, who said, "I found a boy choking on a gibbet in the forest. He was too young to hang so, and I cut him down."

"Indeed? Well, no matter," said the Baron indifferently.

His nonchalance angered Kane. "If his survival is of so little consequence," he demanded, "why was the poor wretch treated so at all?"

"These are my lands. Do not question my laws here!" The Baron's whisper was vicious as a snake's hiss. "And do not think that my laws are so easily flouted," he said ominously.

He turned to the shadows beyond the tide of firelight. "Ah, Kurt." Kane had not heard the old man return, nor any sound that might have hinted at the nature of his task. "Tonight I will dine with my guests," the Baron said.

Then, with a leap of theme that made Kane suspect madness, he demanded of the Puritan: "So you came in search of evil, eh? No other reason? None at all?" His voice sounded both menacing and disturbingly wistful.

"None," Kane said quietly.

"I suppose I must believe you. You will lodge tonight in the Castle Von Staler," he said in a tone that made it unwise to refuse.

Kurt ushered the Englishmen upstairs. Two passages led from the wide landing. One, which was wholly dark, he avoided, and guided them down the second, infrequently lit corridor. He lit torches in brackets outside rooms facing across the corridor, and withdrew.

Though Kane's apartment was crowded with furniture, it was so large as to seem bare. The curtains of the great four-poster were damp and, in places, stained. The tapestries that cloaked the walls were ashen and blurred with dust. Some of the heavy furniture smelled of pine, and seemed in danger of decaying. Two of the men-at-arms entered, bearing logs, and built a fire in the deep hearth. Even the generous flames could not rid the apartment of the sense of decay that pervaded the castle.

Silent appeared, shivering perhaps from the chill of the passage. "By the holy saints, Kane," he muttered, "there's deviltry here. D'ye think as I do, that he has a wench locked up?"

"Aye, mayhap. Or mayhap she has a sickness, and keeps to her rooms."

Silent shook his head and made to speak; then he swore savagely. "Blast the man, he's got me afraid to speak my mind! I feel he can hear me through yon stout wood door!"

They were staring morosely at the fire, and Kane was musing on their ill-defined dilemma, when Kurt announced the Baron's summons. In the hall, the mountainous fire flung shadows behind the long laden table and heavy carved chairs. Counting quickly, Kane saw that places had been set for the Baron, his guests, and the men-at-arms—but for nobody else.

The Baron motioned his guests to sit on either side of him. His eyes were bright, nervous with firelight. At a word, Kurt ushered in the men-at-arms, bearing an entire cooked wild boar. Their stealth made Kane uneasy; apart from Kurt, they seemed to have less presence than specters.

The Baron sampled the meat approvingly. "Well done, Kurt." To his guests he explained: "We have no servants here. They are too loud and too inquisitive."

Kurt filled a plate with choice portions of food and carried it upstairs. "My friends, you are agog to have this mystery solved," the Baron said smiling. "It shall be done. Kurt has taken the plate to the Baroness, who keeps to her rooms."

"Is she unwell?" Kane asked.

"By no means. She is perfect. But none may look upon her."

The bald head turned to Kane, then to Silent. "Those who venture near this castle do so to look upon her perfection," the Baron muttered. "Still, I believe that such is not your mission. It would be ill if it were so, for those who dare must perish. So the youth whom you found on the gibbet learned, as you saw."

Kane was silent, brooding on this unfamiliar evil. His companion said "But why do you hoard such perfection, Baron, for your eyes alone?"

"Not for these eyes, my friend." Smiling bitterly, the Baron touched his eyes, out of which flames glanced. "They see nothing at all."

For the rest of the meal Kane could hardly bear to look at the bright empty eyes; they seemed soulless as the castle. The Baron chatted throughout the meal, and afterward told them of his hunting exploits, though in a bitter tone. But Kane was constantly aware that he was listening to sounds elsewhere in the castle.

At last he bade Kurt show the Englishmen to their apartments. He stood before the hearth, hands stretched out to the fire, as though the fierce heat might conjure back the sight of the flames. Kurt led the men to their doors, and hesitated. "Do not judge my master too harshly," he said in a whisper they had to strain to hear.

He seemed willing to say more. Kane gestured him into his room, and closed the door carefully. The room was chill, despite the fire; he thrust logs into the flames. "Then tell us what possesses him," he demanded low.

"He was not always as you see him. Once he was a great huntsman. Then one day, chasing a boar, his favorite steed threw him. The fall damaged his brain —it robbed him of his sight. That changed him utterly. You saw what he did to his steed."

Kane remembered the blinded horse, and his face grew hot with fury. "But he has never mistreated us," Kurt said hastily. "Before his ill luck, he was the noblest lord of the Black Forest. While others persecuted the peasants for their beliefs, my master offered them sanctuary on his lands, whatever their creeds, and was willing to protect that sanctuary. We who are loyal to him are some of those men, or their sons. The peasants admire him, or fear him. They know nothing of his blindness."

"And what of the woman who cannot be seen?" Silent demanded. "Is she here from choice, as you are?"

Momentarily the faith in the old man's eyes flickered. "She will come to no harm," he said curtly. Before he could be questioned further, he withdrew.

"Name of the Devil, Kane," Silent mouthed, "there's

a prisoner in this castle to be set free, and I'll not sleep until it's done." The parting of his lips made more sound than his whisper. "Are you game to help me?"

"Aye," Kane replied. "But we must be stealthy as shadows."

"I've tracked savages through jungle without their hearing me," his companion said, with a silent laugh.

They eased open the door of the room and crept to the top of the stairs. The Baron sat before the sinking fire, apparently asleep. Otherwise the hall was deserted.

Silent lifted a torch and explored the lightless passage, while Kane returned to the passage from which their apartments opened, to search its depths. Kane's unshod feet had grown almost used to the bare stone. But the dank chill of the reaches of the passage seized him. The doors of the further apartments seemed to have rotted away; the doorways gaped. Within, framed paintings on the walls were black as mud; furniture was overgrown with dust and fungus. The sense of death was claustrophobic here, and he was glad to retreat to his room, having found nothing.

Silent was standing by the fire, as close to the warmth as he could manage. His face looked pale and drawn; his eyes gleamed uneasily. "By God, I heard her," he whispered. "She's there, in a room at the end of that dark corridor. She was singing to herself. I've never heard anything so beautiful, or so lonely."

Kane could see that the incident had disturbed him. But Silent rallied now that his companion had returned. "Pray God her door is not locked," he whispered. "I did not dare to try it, lest the blind one awake. D'ye think we can smuggle her out of this place without wakening him?"

"I think not," the Baron said beyond the door.

His whisper reached into the room like chill drifting mist. Kane snarled, and leaped for the door. But he fell back, for ten of the Baron's men waited there, swords drawn.

The Baron stood among his men. His vicious smile made one side of his face look palsied; his eyes were dead. "You have taught me a lesson, Solomon Kane," he said softly. "My ears can deceive me. I thought you were a man of honor, not a common thief who preys on men's hospitality."

Kane started, ready to match wits with the man if he could. The swords drove him back. "Pray go to your window," the Baron whispered smiling. "I have prepared a spectacle for you."

Beneath the window was an inner courtyard. Dismayed, Kane saw that from a bracket protruding from the opposite wall dangled a hangman's noose. The Baron appeared in the courtyard. Smiling crookedly, he gestured like a conjuror. At once two men-at-arms dragged a youth into view. It was the boy whom Kane had saved from the gibbet.

"Did I not say that my laws would not be flouted?" The Baron sneered at Kane's gasp of rage. "Why, this fellow was brought back to me before you arrived here."

He gestured the men to begin. They obeyed at once, efficiently. Though the boy struggled and cried out, the noose was quickly about his neck. They hauled on the rope, and he jerked in midair, choking.

"See how he entertains his lord. He sings for me, and dances." The Baron cupped one hand at his ear, the better to hear the choking. "But your crime is greater," he hissed, pointing straight at the Englishmen. "I think you will lose your eyes before you hang. First we must make sure that no gallant knight comes to rescue this criminal," he said, and dragged at the legs of the hanged boy until he died.

When the Baron turned purposefully and entered the castle, Kane knew they had no time to plan. "Quickly," he hissed at Silent. Seizing the unburned end of a blazing log from the fire, he rushed at the men in the doorway.

They crowded forward, swords bristling. But the narrowness of the doorway aided him. No more than two men could enter abreast. The first man fell back, clutching his seared face; the second retreated screaming, his hair ablaze.

Both had dropped their swords. Silent seized one weapon, Kane the other—though Kane had to dodge the whistling slash of a blade, which nonetheless chopped flesh from his shoulder. But it was not his sword-arm, and as he rose his sword ripped open the man's torso. The man slumped against the wall, trying to press the wound together as it poured away his life.

Kane had battled his way into the passage. Two blades hacked toward him, and he saved himself only by falling. But his sword bit deep into one man's sword-arm, and while the other was raising his sword to chop Kane down, Kane impaled him through the groin. He caught up the man's fallen sword with his free hand, which still functioned, though painfully.

Silent had reached the corridor now. One of his adversaries tottered back, trying to gasp through his slashed throat. With a two-handed blow he opened the skull of another. "Kane!" he shouted, alerting the Puritan to the rush of the man-behind him, his sword poised spear-like. Kane dodged aside, and his sword hacked deep into the man's neck, like an axe into a tree.

Kane dropped his second sword, for his injured arm was exhausted. The floor was slippery with blood, which soaked through to his feet. The feeling maddened him, and made him frantic to be done with the fight. He was disturbed too by the fanatical silence of the men. Except for the youth who had screamed, they uttered no sound. The walls resounded with the clash of swords; he would never hear the Baron if the blind man crept behind him.

He whirled. But the man behind him was Kurt, hurrying away down the passage—no doubt to protect his master. The last of the ten was chopping at Silent's blade, trying to break through his guard. Silent knocked the blade aside and thrust his sword into the youth's heart.

"Now to our mission," he said grimly to Kane.

They strode to the top of the stairs. Kurt had not hastened to protect the Baron after all, Kane saw; he was guarding the second corridor, that led to the Baroness' room. The Puritan advanced on him, hoping he would yield; it would grieve him to harm the old man, whose only error was an excess of loyalty.

But the Baron's whisper came hissing upstairs. "Even such indomitable heroes as you will not be able to break down her door. I have the only key."

He stood beside the great hearth. Firelight trembled on the key which he drew into sight by a chain around his neck. No longer was he stooping; he towered like a heroic statue, dwarfing the hearth. A sneer twisted his lips, but his eyes were empty. He had taken a saber from the wall, and brandished it before him.

"If you will not yield up the key willingly," Kane said, "I must take it from you."

The rise of the saber-point was the Baron's only reply. Kane began to descend the stairs. At once the two remaining men-at-arms appeared and rushed at him. But Silent ran his gory blade through one while Kane despatched the other, who reeled backward down the stairs, practically decapitated.

The Baron's sword-point moved as though questing like a snake. Kane felt uneasy, almost dishonorable, for challenging a blind man. Perhaps he could disarm the Baron at once. He stole forward, sword poised— and had to leap back, for the saber had whipped down, cutting flesh from his sword-arm.

He had thought the Baron might hear his approach, but never that his perception could be so accurate. He had no time to marvel, for the blind man came noiselessly at him, and the saber clanged against his sword with a shock that jarred his arm painfully. Before he could recover, the saber sprang toward his neck. He almost fell as he recoiled, and even so, blood gushed from a new slash in his neck.

He tried to hold his ground and to attack, but could

do no more than parry. Feinting helped him not at all, for the Baron ignored such ruses as though he was unaware of them. More disturbingly, he seemed able to anticipate Kane's moves with unnerving accuracy. In his blindness he had developed a sixth sense.

Kane's arm ached from parrying. Again he was forced to retreat, as the saber nicked flesh from his side; had he not fallen back, it would have opened his heart. He observed, as best he might as sweat burned his eyes, that the Baron appeared to be suffering. Though Kane's sword had not touched him, the blind face was clenched and twisted. Yet the violence of his blows did not abate.

But Kane had some purpose in retreating. Beside the staircase, out of sight of Kurt above, Silent waited, sword poised. Kane's retreat would take the Baron within reach. Kane cared little for the ruse—but he had no time for scruples, for the Baron was forcing him back. The blind man's sword-point hissed past his eyes, an inch away. Silent raised his sword, his face purple from holding his breath lest it alert their adversary—and the saber clanged against his blade, slamming it against his jaw and hurling him backward onto the stairs, unconscious.

The Baron's face winced as though he had swallowed poison. But the saber swept viciously at Kane. Taken off guard, the Englishman stumbled against the stairs, and fell. The impact of the fall jarred his sword from his hand. The Baron reared above him and lifted the saber to chop the life from him, wincing again at the clatter of the fallen sword.

At once Kane saw where he was vulnerable. As the Puritan twisted aside beneath the saber, he drew a deep breath and uttered a prolonged savage roar such as might have emerged from the throat of an enormous beast.

The Baron covered his ears with his hands, moaning. He staggered backward, and a chair tripped him. His forehead crashed against the table. Kane seized the fallen saber and advanced on the stunned man. Flickering firelight made the Baron's eyes seem to follow the movements of the blade.

At the top of the stairs Kurt cried "No, in God's name!"

Despite the anguish in the man's voice, and the throbbing of his own sword-arm, Kane hesitated only for a few moments. But in that time the Baron struggled to his feet and stood gazing foolishly about the hall. What his mishap while hunting had done, this fall had undone. His sight had returned, after a fashion.

He stumbled toward the stairs, clumsily as a drunkard or an infant, ignoring both Kane and the fallen weapons. Uncertain now, Kane let him go, and stooped to examine Silent, who was stunned but whole.

He heard Kurt gasp at the spectacle of the sighted Baron. Then there came sounds of a struggle. "No, master," the old man was pleading. "You should rest now. You must grow used to your sight again."

"Stand aside, fool!" Kurt was hurled to the floor. Kane gathered that for some reason, the old man was anxious to prevent his master from seeing the Baroness. He heard the Baron's footsteps floundering down the passage, then the sound of a key fumbling in a lock.

There was a breathless silence. Then the Baron's voice resounded down the passage, cracked and wailing. "Traitors! You have stolen her!"

Kane heard a woman's scream, cut off immediately. Kurt tottered to his feet, sobbing dryly. He was unarmed; the Baron had taken his sword. Before Kane could arm himself and seek upstairs, Kurt had stumbled into the dark passage—but almost at once he emerged, with the sword-point at his throat.

The Baron loomed over him, eyes glaring like ice. "You at least I thought would not betray me," he whispered. "But you took her for yourself and put that thing in her place."

Kurt shook his head helplessly, but made no sound,

not even when the sword thrust between his ribs and
sprouted from his back. His hands clutched the
Baron's shoulders in what might have been an attack
or an embrace. The two men struggled at the edge of
the stairs. Still embraced, they crashed the length of
the stairs to the hall, and lay unmoving.

Kane seized a torch and went in search of the
woman who had screamed. At the end of the dark
passage a door stood open. Soft light flickered within.
He dodged into the room, and halted aghast.

It was a woman's apartment. Delicately embroid-
ered tapestries softened the walls; elaborately woven
lace was spread over the furniture. But dust paled
everything. In a great four-poster, whose hangings
were daintily sewn, a woman lay. A widening stain of
blood from a sword-thrust covered her breast, like an
opening flower.

She was pale, and enormously swollen as a termite
queen. Even in life she would hardly have been able
to move. Her face was aged, its features scarcely dis-
tinguishable amid collapsed fat. A key on a chain was
almost hidden between her massive breasts. But at the
ends of arms like pipes, her hands were small and
delicate.

The sense of death, or of suffocating inertia, was
most powerful in this room. Kane hurried back to the
hall, glad to be free of the lightless passage. The Baron
was dead, his spine broken; but Kurt still had breath
in him, though his eyes were dimming.

"What else could I do?" the old man faltered. "She
was my sister; she had not long been a widow. When
the Baron fell blind I brought her here to nurse him.
He became obsessed with her voice and her touch.
For him she became the most beautiful of all women.
When he grew well, he insisted that she stay. Of
course it was an honor, but he confined her to her
apartment, and she became as you saw. Her mind and
her body grew dull. But how could I have told him?
What else could I do?"

He seemed to be pleading for reassurance. Kane

shook his head sadly, which appeared to satisfy the
old man. And so he died.

Silent regained consciousness snarling, and grabbed
for his sword. Kane told him what had happened; but
he must see for himself. Shortly he returned, his face
ashen. They left the castle and its smell of blood, to
search for the stables, where they found Silent's horse
and a steed for Kane. The other horses they set free.

As dawn reached between the firs, illuminating
tracks of mist, they rode away. Above them trees
closed about the castle, which grew blurred, as though
decay were progressing more swiftly now that all life
was gone. They were glad to reach the forest trail.
They would ride together for awhile, until Silent
headed for the wide sea, while Kane went wandering
again until evil drew him.

THE MOON OF SKULLS

CHAPTER 1
A MAN COMES SEEKING

A great black shadow lay across the land, cleaving the red flame of the sunset. To the man who toiled up the jungle trail it loomed like a symbol of death and horror, a menace brooding and terrible, like the shadow of a stealthy assassin flung upon some candle-lit wall.

Yet it was only the shadow of the great crag which reared up in front of him, the first outpost of the grim foothills which were his goal. He halted a moment at its foot, staring upward where it rose blackly limned against the dying sun. He could have sworn that he caught the hint of a movement at the top, as he stared, hand shielding his eyes, but the fading glare dazzled him and he could not be sure. Was it a man who darted to cover? A man, or—?

- He shrugged his shoulders and fell to examining the rough trail which led up and over the brow of the crag. At first glance it seemed that only a mountain goat could scale it, but closer investigation showed numbers of fingerholds drilled into the solid rock. It would be a task to try his powers to the utmost but he had not come a thousand miles to turn back now.

He dropped the large pouch he wore at his shoulder, and laid down the clumsy musket, retaining only his long rapier, dagger, and one of his pistols. These he strapped behind him, and without a backward glance over the darkening trail he had come, he started the long ascent.

He was a tall man, long-armed and iron-muscled, yet again and again he was forced to halt in his upward climb and rest for a moment, clinging like an ant to the precipitous face of the cliff. Night fell swiftly and the crag above him was a shadowy blur in which he was forced to feel with his fingers, blindly, for the holes which served him as a precarious ladder.

Below him, the night noises of the tropical jungle broke forth, yet it appeared to him that even these sounds were subdued and hushed as though the great black hills looming above threw a spell of silence and fear even over the jungle creatures.

On up he struggled, and now to make his way harder, the cliff bulged outward near its summit, and the strain on nerve and muscle became heartbreaking. Time and again a hold slipped and he escaped falling by a hair's breadth. But every fiber in his lean hard body was perfectly coordinated, and his fingers were like steel talons with the grip of a vise. His progress grew slower and slower but on he went until at last he saw the cliff's brow splitting the stars a scant twenty feet above him.

And even as he looked, a vague bulk heaved into view, toppled on the edge and hurtled down toward him with a great rush of air about it. Flesh crawling, he flattened himself against the cliff's face and felt a heavy blow against his shoulder, only a glancing blow, but even so it nearly tore him from his hold, and as he fought desperately to right himself, he heard a reverberating crash among the rocks far below. Cold sweat beading his brow, he looked up. Who—or what—had shoved that boulder over the cliff edge? He was brave, as the bones on many a battlefield could testify, but the thought of dying like a sheep, helpless and with no chance of resistance, turned his blood cold.

Then a wave of fury supplanted his fear and he renewed his climb with reckless speed. The expected second boulder did not come, however, and no living

thing met his sight as he clambered up over the edge
and leaped erect, sword flashing from its scabbard.

He stood upon a sort of plateau which debouched
into a very broken hilly country some half mile to
the west. The crag he had just mounted jutted out
from the rest of the heights like a sullen promontory,
looming above the sea of waving foliage below, now
dark and mysterious in the tropic night.

Silence ruled here in absolute sovereignty. No
breeze stirred the somber depths below, and no foot-
fall rustled amid the stunted bushes which cloaked
the plateau, yet that boulder which had almost hurled
the climber to his death had not fallen by chance.
What beings moved among these grim hills? The tropical darkness fell about the lone wanderer like a heavy
veil through which the yellow stars blinked evilly. The
steams of the rotting jungle vegetation floated up to
him as tangible as a thick fog, and making a wry face
he strode away from the cliff, heading boldly across
the plateau, sword in one hand and pistol in the other.

There was an uncomfortable feeling of being
watched in the very air. The silence remained un-
broken save for the soft swishing that marked the
stranger's cat-like tread through the tall upland grass,
yet the man sensed that living things glided before
and behind him and on each side. Whether man or
beast trailed him he knew not, nor did he care over-
much, for he was prepared to fight human or devil who
barred his way. Occasionally he halted and glanced
challengingly about him, but nothing met his eye except the shrubs which crouched like short dark ghosts
about his trail, blended and blurred in the thick, hot
darkness through which the very stars seemed to
struggle, redly.

At last he came to the place where the plateau broke
into the higher slopes and there he saw a clump of
trees blocked out solidly in the lesser shadows. He
approached warily, then halted as his gaze, growing
somewhat accustomed to the darkness, made out a

vague form among the somber trunks which was not
a part of them. He hesitated. The figure neither advanced nor fled. A dim form of silent menace, it lurked
as if in wait. A brooding horror hung over that still
cluster of trees.

The stranger advanced warily, blade extended.
Closer. Straining his eyes for some hint of threatening
motion. He decided that the figure was human but he
was puzzled at its lack of movement. Then the reason
became apparent—it was the corpse of a black man
that stood among those trees, held erect by spears
through his body, nailing him to the boles. One arm
was extended in front of him, held in place along a
great branch by a dagger through the wrist, the index
finger straight as if the corpse pointed stiffly—back
along the way the stranger had come.

The meaning was obvious; that mute grim signpost
could have but one significance—death lay beyond.
The man who stood gazing upon that grisly warning
rarely laughed, but now he allowed himself the luxury
of a sardonic smile. A thousand miles of land and sea
—ocean travel and jungle travel—and now they expected to turn him back with such mummery—whoever they were.

He resisted the temptation to salute the corpse, as
an action wanting in decorum, and pushed on boldly
through the grove, half expecting an attack from the
rear or an ambush.

Nothing of the sort occurred, however, and emerg-
ing from the trees, he found himself at the foot of a
rugged incline, the first of a series of slopes. He strode
stolidly upward in the night, nor did he even pause to
reflect how unusual his actions must have appeared
to a sensible man. The average man would have
camped at the foot of the crag and waited for morning
before even attempting to scale the cliffs. But this was
no ordinary man. Once his objective was in sight, he
followed the straightest line to it, without a thought
of obstacles, whether day or night. What was to be
done, must be done. He had reached the outposts of

the kingdom of fear at dusk, and invading its inmost recesses by night seemed to follow as a matter of course.

As he went up the boulder-strewn slopes the moon rose, lending its air of illusion, and in its light the broken hills ahead loomed up like the black spires of wizards' castles. He kept his eyes fixed on the dim trail he was following, for he knew not when another boulder might come hurtling down the inclines. He expected an attack of any sort and, naturally, it was the unexpected which really happened.

Suddenly from behind a great rock stepped a man; an ebony giant in the pale moonlight, a long spear blade gleaming silver in his hand, his headpiece of ostrich plumes floating above him like a white cloud. He lifted the spear in a ponderous salute, and spoke in the dialect of the river-tribes:

"This is not the white man's land. Who is my white brother in his own kraal and why does he come into the Land of Skulls?"

"My name is Solomon Kane," the white man answered in the same language. "I seek the vampire queen of Negari."

"Few seek. Fewer find. None return," answered the other cryptically.

"Will you lead me to her?"

"You bear a long dagger in your right hand. There are no lions here."

"A serpent dislodged a boulder. I thought to find snakes in the bushes."

The giant acknowledged this interchange of subtleties with a grim smile and a brief silence fell.

"Your life," said the black man presently, "is in my hand."

Kane smiled thinly. "I carry the lives of many warriors in my hand."

The negro's gaze traveled uncertainly up and down the shimmery length of the Englishman's sword. Then he shrugged his mighty shoulders and let his spear point sink to the earth.

"You bear no gifts," said he; "but follow me and I will lead you to the Terrible One, the Mistress of Doom, the Red Woman, Nakari, who rules the land of Negari."

He stepped aside and motioned Kane to precede him, but the Englishman, his mind on a spear-thrust in the back, shook his head.

"Who am I that I should walk in front of my brother? We be two chiefs—let us walk side by side."

In his heart Kane railed that he should be forced to use such unsavory diplomacy with a savage warrior, but he showed no sign. The giant bowed with a certain barbaric majesty and together they went up the hill trail, unspeaking. Kane was aware that men were stepping from hiding places and falling in behind them, and a surreptitious glance over his shoulder showed him some two score warriors trailing out behind them in two wedge-shaped lines. The moonlight glittered on sleek bodies, on waving headgears and long, cruel spear blades.

"My brothers are like leopards," said Kane courteously; "they lie in the low bushes and no eyes see them; they steal through the high grass and no man hears their coming."

The black chief acknowledged the compliment with a courtly inclination of his lion-like head, that set the plumes whispering.

"The mountain leopard is our brother, oh chieftain. Our feet are like drifting smoke but our arms are like iron. When they strike, blood drips red and men die."

Kane sensed an undercurrent of menace in the tone. There was no actual hint of threat on which he might base his suspicions, but the sinister minor note was there. He said no more for a space and the strange band moved silently upward in the moonlight like a cavalcade of specters.

The trail grew steeper and more rocky, winding in and out among crags and gigantic boulders. Suddenly a great chasm opened before them, spanned by a natural bridge of rock, at the foot of which the leader halted.

Kane stared at the abyss curiously. It was some forty feet wide, and looking down, his gaze was swallowed by impenetrable blackness, hundreds of feet deep, he knew. On the other side rose crags dark and forbidding.

"Here," said the chief, "begin the true borders of Nakari's realm."

Kane was aware that the warriors were casually closing in on him. His fingers instinctively tightened about the hilt of the rapier which he had not sheathed. The air was suddenly super-charged with tension.

"Here, too," the warrior chief said, "they who bring no gifts to Nakari—die!"

The last word was a shriek, as if the thought had transformed the speaker into a maniac, and as he screamed it, the great arm went back and then forward with a ripple of mighty muscles, and the long spear leaped at Kane's breast.

Only a born fighter could have avoided that thrust. Kane's instinctive action saved his life—the great blade grazed his ribs as he swayed aside and returned the blow with a flashing thrust that killed a warrior who jostled between him and the chief at that instant.

Spears flashed in the moonlight and Kane, parrying one and bending under the thrust of another, sprang out upon the narrow bridge where only one could come at him at a time.

None cared to be first. They stood upon the brink and thrust at him, crowding forward when he retreated, giving back when he pressed them. Their spears were longer than his rapier but he more than made up for the difference and the great odds by his scintillant skill and the cold ferocity of his attack.

They wavered back and forth and then suddenly a giant leaped from among his fellows and charged out upon the bridge like a wild buffalo, shoulders hunched, spear held low, eyes gleaming with a look not wholly sane. Kane leaped back before the onslaught, leaped back again, striving to avoid that stabbing spear and to find an opening for his point. He sprang to one side and found himself reeling on the edge of the bridge with eternity gaping beneath him. The warriors yelled in savage exultation as he swayed and fought for his balance, and the giant on the bridge roared and plunged at his rocking foe.

Kane parried with all his strength—a feat few swordsmen could have accomplished, off balance as he was—saw the cruel spear blade flash by his cheek —felt himself falling backward into the abyss. A desperate effort, and he gripped the spear shaft, righted himself and ran the spearman through the body. The giant's great red cavern of a mouth spouted blood and with a dying effort he hurled himself blindly against his foe. Kane, with his heels over the bridge's edge, was unable to avoid him and they toppled over together, to disappear silently into the depths below.

So swiftly had it all happened that the warriors stood stunned. The giant's roar of triumph had scarcely died on his lips before the two were falling into the darkness. Now the rest of the natives came out on the bridge to peer down curiously, but no sound came up from the dark void.

CHAPTER 2

THE PEOPLE OF THE STALKING DEATH

As Kane fell he followed his fighting instinct, twisting in midair so that when he struck, were it ten or a thousand feet below, he would land on top of the man who fell with him.

The end came suddenly—much more suddenly than the Englishman had thought for. He lay half stunned for an instant, then looking up, saw dimly the narrow bridge banding the sky above him, and the forms of the warriors, limned in the moonlight and grotesquely foreshortened as they leaned over the edge. He lay still, knowing that the beams of the moon did not pierce the deeps in which he was hidden, and that to those watchers he was invisible. Then when they vanished from view he began to review his present plight. His opponent was dead, and only for the fact that his corpse had cushioned the fall, Kane would have been dead likewise, for they had fallen a considerable distance. As it was, the Englishman was stiff and bruised.

He drew his sword from the native's body, thankful that it had not been broken, and began to grope about in the darkness. His hand encountered the edge of what seemed a cliff. He had thought that he was on the bottom of the chasm and that its impression of great depth had been a delusion, but now he decided that he had fallen on a ledge, part of the way down. He dropped a small stone over the side, and after what seemed a very long time he heard the faint sound of its striking far below.

Somewhat at a loss as to how to proceed, he drew flint and steel from his belt and struck them to some tinder, warily shielding the light with his hands. The faint illumination showed a large ledge jutting out from the side of the cliff, that is, the side next the hills, to which he had been attempting to cross. He had fallen close to the edge and it was only by the narrowest margin that he had escaped sliding off it, not knowing his position.

Crouching there, his eyes seeking to accustom themselves to the abysmal gloom, he made out what seemed to be a darker shadow in the shadows of the wall. On closer examination he found it to be an opening large enough to admit his body standing erect. A cavern, he assumed, and though its appearance was dark and forbidding in the extreme, he entered, groping his way when the tinder burned out.

Where it led to, he naturally had no idea, but any action was preferable to sitting still until the mountain vultures plucked his bones. For a long way the cave floor tilted upward—solid rock beneath his feet—and Kane made his way with some difficulty up the rather steep slant, slipping and sliding now and then. The cavern seemed a large one, for at no time after entering it could he touch the roof, nor could he, with a hand on one wall, reach the other.

At last the floor became level and Kane sensed that the cave was much larger there. The air seemed better, though the darkness was just as impenetrable. Suddenly he stopped dead in his tracks. From somewhere in front of him there came a strange indescribable rustling. Without warning something smote him in the face and slashed wildly. All about him sounded the eery murmurings of many small wings and suddenly Kane smiled crookedly, amused, relieved and chagrined. Bats, of course. The cave was swarming with them. Still, it was a shaky experience, and as he went on and the wings whispered through the vast emptiness of the great cavern, Kane's Puritan mind found space to dally with a bizarre thought—had he wandered into Hell by some strange means, and were these in truth bats, or were they lost souls winging through everlasting night?

Then, thought Solomon Kane, I will soon confront Satan himself—and even as he thought this, his nostrils were assailed by a horrid scent, fetid and repellent. The scent grew as he went slowly on, and Kane swore softly, though he was not a profane man. He sensed that the smell betokened some hidden threat, some unseen malevolence, inhuman and deathly, and his somber mind sprang at supernatural conclusions. However, he felt perfect confidence in his ability to cope with any fiend or demon, armored as he was in unshakable faith of creed and the knowledge of the rightness of his cause.

What followed happened suddenly. He was groping his way along when in front of him two narrow yellow eyes leaped up in the darkness—eyes that were cold and expressionless, too hideously close-set for human eyes and too high for any four-legged beast. What horror had thus reared itself up in front of him?

This is Satan, thought Kane as the eyes swayed above him, and the next instant he was battling for his life with the darkness that seemed to have taken tangible form and thrown itself about his body and limbs in great slimy coils. Those coils lapped his sword arm and rendered it useless; with the other hand he groped for dagger or pistol, flesh crawling as his fingers slipped from slick scales, while the hissing of the monster filled the cavern with a cold paean of terror.

There in the black dark to the accompaniment of the bats' leathery rustlings, Kane fought like a rat in the grip of a mouse-snake, and he could feel his ribs giving and his breath going before his frantic left hand closed on his dagger hilt.

Then with a volcanic twist and wrench of his steel-thewed body he tore his left arm partly free and plunged the keen blade again and again to the hilt in the sinuous writhing terror which enveloped him, feeling at last the quivering coils loosen and slide from his limbs to lie about his feet like huge cables.

The mighty serpent lashed wildly in its death struggles, and Kane, avoiding its bone-shattering blows, reeled away in the darkness, laboring for breath. If his antagonist had not been Satan himself, it had been Satan's nearest earthly satellite, thought Solomon, hoping devoutly that he would not be called upon to battle another in the darkness there.

It seemed to him that he had been walking through the blackness for ages and he began to wonder if there were any end to the cave when a glimmer of light pierced the darkness. He thought it to be an outer entrance a great way off, and started forward swiftly, but to his astonishment, he brought up short against a blank wall after taking a few strides.

Then he perceived that the light came through a narrow crack in the wall, and feeling over this wall he found it to be of different material from the rest of the cave, consisting, apparently, of regular blocks of stone joined together with mortar of some sort—an indubitably man-built wall.

The light streamed between two of these stones where the mortar had crumbled away. Kane ran his hands over the surface with an interest beyond his present needs. The work seemed very old and very much superior to what might be expected of a tribe of ignorant savages.

He felt the thrill of the explorer and discoverer. Certainly no white man had ever seen this place and lived to tell of it, for when he had landed on the dank West Coast some months before, preparing to plunge into the interior, he had had no hint of such a country as this. The few white men who knew anything at all of Africa with whom he had talked, had never even mentioned the Land of Skulls, or the she-fiend who ruled it.

Kane thrust against the wall cautiously. The structure seemed weakened from age—a vigorous shove and it gave perceptibly. He hurled himself against it with all his weight and a whole section of wall gave way with a crash, precipitating him into a dimly lighted corridor amid a heap of stone, dust and mortar.

He sprang up and looked about, expecting the noise to bring a horde of wild spearmen. Utter silence reigned. The corridor in which he now stood was much like a long narrow cave itself, save that it was the work of man. It was several feet wide and the roof was many feet above his head. Dust lay ankle-deep on the floor as if no foot had trod there for countless centuries, and the dim light, Kane decided, filtered in somehow through the roof or ceiling, for nowhere did he see any doors or windows. At last he decided the source was the ceiling itself, which was of a peculiar phosphorescent quality.

He set off down the corridor, feeling uncomfortably like a gray ghost moving along the gray halls of death and decay. The evident antiquity of his surroundings depressed him, making him sense vaguely the fleeting and futile existence of mankind. That he was now on top of the earth he believed, since light of a sort came in, but where, he could not even offer a conjecture. This was a land of enchantment—a land of horror and fearful mysteries, the jungle and river natives had said, and he had gotten whispered hints of its terrors ever since he had set his back to the Slave Coast and ventured into the hinterlands alone.

Now and then he caught a low indistinct murmur which seemed to come through one of the walls, and he at last came to the conclusion that he had stumbled onto a secret passage in some castle or house. The natives who had dared speak to him of Negari, had whispered of a ju-ju city built of stone, set high amid the grim black crags of the fetish hills.

Then, thought Kane, it may be that I have blundered upon the very thing I sought and am in the midst of that city of terror. He halted, and choosing a place at random, began to loosen the mortar with his dagger. As he worked he again heard that low murmur, increasing in volume as he bored through the wall, and presently the point pierced through, and looking through the aperture it had made, he saw a strange and fantastic scene.

He was looking into a great chamber, whose walls and floor were of stone, and whose mighty roof was upheld by gigantic stone columns, strangely carved. Ranks of feathered black warriors lined the walls and a double column of them stood like statues before a throne set between two stone dragons which were larger than elephants. These men he recognized, by their bearing and general appearance, to be tribesmen of the warriors he had fought at the chasm. But his gaze was drawn irresistibly to the great, grotesquely ornamented throne. There, dwarfed by the ponderous splendor about her, a woman reclined. A tawny woman she was, young and of a tigerish comeliness. She was naked except for a beplumed helmet, armbands, anklets and a girdle of colored ostrich feathers, and she sprawled upon the silken cushions with her limbs thrown about in voluptous abandon.

Even at that distance Kane could make out that her features were regal yet barbaric, haughty and imperious, yet sensual, and with a touch of ruthless cruelty about the curl of full red lips. Kane felt his pulse quicken. This could be no other than she whose crimes had become almost mythical—Nakari of Negari, demon queen of a demon city, whose monstrous lust for blood had set half a continent shivering.

At least she seemed human enough; the tales of the fearful river tribes had lent her a supernatural aspect. Kane had half expected to see a loathsome semi-human monster out of some past and demoniacal age.

The Englishman gazed, fascinated though repelled. Not even in the courts of Europe had he seen such grandeur. The chamber and all its accouterments, from the carven serpents twined about the bases of the pillars to the dimly seen dragons on the shadowy ceiling, were fashioned on a gigantic scale. The splendor was awesome—elephantine—inhumanly oversized, and almost numbing to the mind which sought to measure and conceive the magnitude thereof. To Kane it seemed that these things must have been the work of gods rather than men, for this chamber alone would dwarf most of the castles he had known in Europe.

The fighting men who thronged that mighty room seemed grotesquely incongruous. They were not the architects of that ancient place.

As Kane realized this the sinister importance of Queen Nakari dwindled. Sprawled on that august throne in the midst of the terrific glory of another age, she seemed to assume her true proportions—a spoiled, petulant child engaged in a game of make-believe and using for her sport a toy discarded by her elders. And at the same time a thought entered Kane's mind— who were these elders?

Still, the child could become deadly in her game, as the Englishman soon saw.

A tall and massive warrior came through the ranks fronting the throne, and after prostrating himself four times before it, remained on his knees, evidently awaiting permission to speak. The queen's air of lazy indifference fell from her and she straightened with a quick lithe motion that reminded Kane of a leopardess springing erect. She spoke, and the words came faintly to him as he strained his faculties to hear. She spoke in a language very similar to that of the river tribes.

"Speak!"

"Great and Terrible One," said the kneeling warrior, and Kane recognized him as the chief who had first accosted him on the plateau—the chief of the guards on the cliffs, "let not the fire of your fury consume your slave."

The young woman's eyes narrowed viciously.

"You know why you were summoned, son of a vulture?"

"Fire of Beauty, the stranger called Kane brought no gifts."

"No gifts?" she spat out the words. "What have I to do with gifts?"

The chief hesitated, knowing now that there was some special importance in this stranger.

"Gazelle of Negari, he came climbing the crags in the night like an assassin, with a dagger as long as a man's arm in his hand. The boulder we hurled down missed him, and we met him upon the plateau and took him to the Bridge-Across-the-Sky, where, as is the custom, we thought to slay him; for it was your word that you were weary of men who came wooing you."

"Fool," she snarled. "Fool!"

"Your slave did not know, Queen of Beauty. The strange man fought like a mountain leopard. Two men he slew and fell with the last one into the chasm, and so he perished, Star of Negari."

"Aye," the queen's tone was venomous. "The first great man who ever came to Negari! One who might have—rise, fool!"

The man got to his feet.

"Mighty Lioness, might not this one have come seeking—"

The sentence was never completed. Even as he straightened, Nakari made a swift gesture with her hand. Two warriors plunged from the silent ranks and two spears crossed in the chief's body before he could turn. A gurgling scream burst from his lips, blood spurted high in the air and the corpse fell flatly at the foot of the great throne.

The ranks never wavered, but Kane caught the sidelong flash of strangely red eyes and the involuntary wetting of thick lips. Nakari had half risen as the spears flashed, and now she sank back, an expression of cruel satisfaction on her beautiful face and a strange brooding gleam in her scintillant eyes.

An indifferent wave of her hand and the corpse was dragged away by the heels, the dead arms trailing limply in the wide smear of blood left by the passage of the body. Kane could see other wide stains crossing the stone floor, some almost indistinct, others less dim. How many wild scenes of blood and cruel frenzy had the great stone throne-dragons looked upon with their carven eyes?

He did not doubt, now, the tales told him by the river tribes. These people were bred in rapine and horror. Their prowess had burst their brains. They lived, like some terrible beasts, only to destroy. There were strange gleams behind their eyes which at times lit those eyes with up-leaping flames and shadows of Hell. What had the river tribes said of these mountain people who had ravaged them for countless centuries? That "they were henchmen of death, who stalked among them, and whom they worshipped."

Still the thought hovered in Kane's mind as he watched—who built this place, and why were these people evidently in possession? Fighting men such as they were could not have reached the culture evidenced by these carvings. Yet the river tribes had spoken of no other men than those upon which he now looked.

The Englishman tore himself away from the fascination of the barbaric scene with an effort. He had no time to waste; as long as they thought him dead, he had more chance of eluding possible guards and seeking what he had come to find. He turned and set off down the dim corridor. No plan of action offered itself to his mind and one direction was as good as another. The passage did not run straight; it turned and twisted, following the line of the walls, Kane supposed, and found time to wonder at the evident enormous thickness of those walls. He expected at any moment to meet some guard or slave, but as the corridors continued to stretch empty before him, with the dusty floors unmarked by any footprint, he decided that either the passages were unknown to the people of Negari or else for some reason were never used.

He kept a close lookout for secret doors, and at last found one, made fast on the inner side with a rusty bolt set in a groove of the wall. This he manipulated cautiously, and presently with a creaking which seemed terrifically loud in the stillness the door swung inward. Looking out he saw no one, and stepping warily through the opening, he drew the door to behind him, noting that it assumed the part of a fantastic picture painted on the wall. He scraped a mark with his dagger at the point where he believed the hidden spring to be on the outer side, for he knew not when he might need to use the passage again.

He was in a great hall, through which ran a maze of giant pillars much like those of the throne chamber. Among them he felt like a child in some great forest, yet they gave him some slight sense of security since he believed that, gliding among them like a ghost through a jungle, he could elude the warriors in spite of their craft.

He set off, choosing his direction at random and going carefully. Once he heard a mutter of voices, and leaping upon the base of a column, clung there while two women passed directly beneath him, but besides these he encountered no one. It was an uncanny sensation, passing through this vast hall which seemed empty of human life, but in some other part of which Kane knew there might be throngs of people, hidden from sight by the pillars.

At last, after what seemed an eternity of following these monstrous mazes, he came upon a huge wall which seemed to be either a side of the hall, or a partition, and continuing along this, he saw in front of him a doorway before which two spearmen stood like black statues.

Kane, peering about the corner of a column base, made out two windows high in the wall, one on each side of the door, and noting the ornate carvings which covered the walls, determined on a desperate plan.

He felt it imperative that he should see what lay within that room. The fact that it was guarded suggested that the room beyond the door was either a treasure chamber or a dungeon, and he felt sure that his ultimate goal would prove to be a dungeon.

Kane retreated to a point out of sight of the guards and began to scale the wall, using the deep carvings for hand and foot holds. It proved even easier than he had hoped, and having climbed to a point level with the windows, he crawled cautiously along a horizontal line, feeling like an ant on a wall.

The guards far below him never looked up, and finally he reached the nearer window and drew himself up over the sill. He looked down into a large room, empty of life, but equipped in a manner sensuous and barbaric. Silken couches and velvet cushions dotted the floor in profusion, and tapestries heavy with gold work hung upon the walls. The ceiling too was worked in gold.

Strangely incongruous, crude trinkets of ivory and ironwood, unmistakably savage in workmanship, lit-

tered the place, symbolic enough of this strange kingdom where signs of barbarism vied with a strange
culture. The outer door was shut and in the wall opposite was another door, also closed.

Kane descended from the window, sliding down the
edge of a tapestry as a sailor slides down a sail-rope,
and crossed the room. His feet sank noiselessly into the
deep fabric of the rug which covered the floor, and
which, like all the other furnishings, seemed ancient
to the point of decay.

At the door he hesitated. To step into the next room
might be a desperately hazardous thing to do; should
it prove to be filled with warriors, his escape was cut
off by the spearmen outside the other door. Still, he
was used to taking all sorts of wild chances, and now,
sword in hand, he flung the door open with a suddenness intended to numb with surprise for an instant any
foe who might be on the other side.

Kane took a swift step within, ready for anything—
then halted suddenly, struck speechless and motionless
for a second. He had come thousands of miles in search
of something, and there before him lay the object of
his search.

CHAPTER 3

LILITH

A couch stood in the middle of the room, and on its
silken surface lay a woman—a woman whose skin was
fair and whose reddish gold hair fell about her bare
shoulders. She now sprang erect, fright flooding her
fine gray eyes, lips parted to utter a cry which she as
suddenly checked.

"You!" she exclaimed. "How did you—?"

Solomon Kane closed the door behind him and came
toward her, a rare smile on his dark face.

"You remember me, do you not, Marylin?"

The fear had already faded from her eyes even

before he spoke, to be replaced by a look of incredible
wonder and dazed bewilderment.

"Captain Kane! I can not understand—it seemed
no one would ever come—"

She drew a small hand wearily across her brow,
swaying suddenly.

Kane caught her in his arms—she was only a child
—and laid her gently on the couch. There, chafing her
wrists gently, he talked in a low hurried monotone,
keeping an eye on the door all the time—which door,
by the way, seemed to be the only entrance or egress
from the room. While he talked he mechanically took
in the chamber, noting that it was almost a duplicate
of the outer room as regards hangings and general
furnishings.

"First," said he, "before we go into any other matters, tell me, are you closely guarded?"

"Very closely, sir," she murmured hopelessly; "I
know not how you came here, but we can never
escape."

"Let me tell you swiftly how I came to be here,
and mayhap you will be more hopeful when I tell you
of the difficulties already overcome. Lie still now,
Marylin, and I will tell you how I came to seek an
English heiress in the devil city of Negari.

"I killed Sir John Taferal in a duel. As to the reason,
'tis neither here nor there, but slander and a black lie
lay behind it. Ere he died he confessed that he had
committed a foul crime some years agone. You remember, of course, the affection cherished for you by your
cousin, old Lord Hildred Taferal, Sir John's uncle?
Sir John feared that the old lord, dying without issue,
might leave the great Taferal estates to you.

"Years ago you disappeared and Sir John spread the
rumor that you had drowned. Yet when he lay dying
with my rapier through his body, he gasped out that
he had kidnapped you and sold you to a Barbary
rover, whom he named—a bloody pirate whose name
has not been unknown on England's coasts aforetime.

So I came seeking you, and a long weary trail it has been, stretching into long leagues and bitter years.

"First I sailed the seas searching for El Gar, the Barbary corsair named by Sir John. I found him in the crash and roar of an ocean battle; he died, but even as he lay dying he told me that he had sold you in turn to a merchant out of Stamboul. So to the Levant I went and there by chance came upon a Greek sailor whom the Moors had crucified on the shore for piracy. I cut him down and asked him the question I asked all men—if he had in his wanderings seen a captive English girl-child with yellow curls. I learned that he had been one of the crew of the Stamboul merchant, and that she had, on her homeward voyage, been set upon by a Portuguese slaver and sunk—this renegade Greek and the child being among the few who were taken aboard the slaver.

"This slaver then, cruising south for black ivory, had been ambushed in a small bay on the African West Coast, and of your further fate the Greek knew nothing, for he had escaped the general massacre, and taking to sea in an open boat, had been taken up by a ship of Genoese freebooters.

"To the West Coast, then, I came, on the slim chance that you still lived, and there heard among the natives that some years ago a white child had been taken from a ship whose crew had been slain, and sent inland as a part of the tribute the shore tribes paid to the upper river chiefs.

"Then all traces ceased. For months I wandered without a clue as to your whereabouts, nay, without a hint that you even lived. Then I chanced to hear among the river tribes of the demon city of Negari and the evil queen who kept a foreign woman for a slave. I came here."

Kane's matter-of-fact tone, his unfurbished narration, gave no hint of the full meaning of that tale—of what lay behind those calm and measured words—the sea fights and the land fights—the years of privation and heart-breaking toil, the ceaseless danger, the ever-lasting wandering through hostile and unknown lands, the tedious and deadening labor of ferreting out the information he wished from ignorant, sullen and un-friendly savages.

"I came here," said Kane simply, but what a world of courage and effort was symbolized by that phrase! A long red trail, black shadows and crimson shadows weaving a devil's dance—marked by flashing swords and the smoke of battle—by faltering words falling like drops of blood from the lips of dying men.

Not a consciously dramatic man, certainly, was Solomon Kane. He told his tale in the same manner in which he had overcome terrific obstacles—coldly, briefly and without heroics.

"You see, Marylin," he concluded gently, "I have not come this far and done this much, to now meet with defeat. Take heart, child. We will find a way out of this fearful place."

"Sir John took me on his saddlebow," the girl said dazedly, and speaking slowly as if her native language came strangely to her from years of unuse, as she framed in halting words an English evening of long ago: "He carried me to the seashore where a galley's boat waited, filled with fierce men, dark and mus-tached and having scimitars, and great rings to the fingers. The captain, a Moslem with a face like a hawk, took me, I a-weeping with fear, and bore me to his galley. Yet he was kind to me in his way, I being little more than a baby, and at last sold me to a Turkish merchant, as he told you. This merchant he met off the southern coast of France, after many days of sea travel.

"This man did not use me badly, yet I feared him, for he was a man of cruel countenance and made me understand that I was to be sold to a black sultan of the Moors. However, in the Gates of Hercules his ship was set upon by a Cadiz slaver and things came about as you have said.

"The captain of the slaver believed me to be the

child of some wealthy English family and intended holding me for ransom, but in a grim darksome bay on the African coast he perished with all his men except the Greek you have mentioned, and I was taken captive by a savage chieftain.

"I was terribly afraid and thought he would slay me, but he did me no harm and sent me up-country with an escort, who also bore much loot taken from the ship. This loot, together with myself, was, as you know, intended for a powerful king of the river peoples. But it never reached him, for a roving band of Negari fell upon the beach warriors and slew them all. Then I was taken to this city, and have since remained, slave to Queen Nakari.

"How I have lived through all those terrible scenes of battle and cruelty and murder, I know not."

"A providence has watched over you, child," said Kane, "the power which doth care for weak women and helpless children; which led me to you in spite of all hindrances, and which shall yet lead us forth from this place, God willing."

"My people!" she exclaimed suddenly like one awaking from a dream; "what of them?"

"All in good health and fortune, child, save that they have sorrowed for you through the long years. Nay, old Sir Hildred hath the gout and doth so swear thereat that I fear for his soul at times. Yet methinks that the sight of you, little Marylin, would mend him."

"Still, Captain Kane," said the girl, "I can not understand why you came alone."

"Your brothers would have come with me, child, but it was not sure that you lived, and I was loth that any other Taferal should die in a land far from good English soil. I rid the country of an evil Taferal—'twas but just I should restore in his place a good Taferal, if so be she still lived—I, and I alone."

This explanation Kane himself believed. He never sought to analyze his motives and he never wavered once his mind was made up. Though he always acted on impulse, he firmly believed that all his actions were

governed by cold and logical reasonings. He was a
man born out of his time—a strange blending of Puritan and Cavalier, with a touch of the ancient philos-
opher, and more than a touch of the pagan, though
the last assertion would have shocked him unspeak-
ably. An atavist of the days of blind chivalry he was,
a knight errant in the somber clothes of a fanatic. A
hunger in his soul drove him on and on, an urge to
right all wrongs, protect all weaker things, avenge all
crimes against right and justice. Wayward and restless
as the wind, he was consistent in only one respect—he
was true to his ideals of justice and right. Such was
Solomon Kane.

"Marylin," he now said kindly, taking her small
hands in his sword-calloused fingers, "methinks you
have changed greatly in the years. You were a rosy
and chubby little maid when I used to dandle you on
my knee in old England. Now you seem drawn and
pale of face, though you are beautiful as the nymphs
of the heathen books. There are haunting ghosts in
your eyes, child—do they misuse you here?"

She lay back on the couch and the blood drained
slowly from her already pallid features until she was
deathly white. Kane bent over her, startled. Her voice
came in a whisper.

"Ask me not. There are deeds better hidden in the
darkness of night and forgetfulness. There are sights
which blast the eyes and leave their burning mark
forever on the brain. The walls of ancient cities, recked
not of by men, have looked upon scenes not to be
spoken of, even in whispers."

Her eyes closed wearily and Kane's troubled, somber
eyes unconsciously traced the thin blue lines of her
veins, prominent against the unnatural whiteness of
her skin.

"Here is some demoniacal thing," he muttered. "A
mystery—"

"Aye," murmured the girl, "a mystery that was old
when Egypt was young! And nameless evil more

ancient than dark Babylon—that spawned in terrible black cities when the world was young and strange."

Kane frowned, troubled. At the girl's strange words he felt an eery crawling fear at the back of his brain, as if dim racial memories stirred in the eon-deep gulfs, conjuring up grim chaotic visions, illusive and nightmarish.

Suddenly Marylin sat erect, her eyes flaring wide with fright. Kane heard a door open somewhere.

"Nakari!" whispered the girl urgently. "Swift! She must not find you here! Hide quickly, and"—as Kane turned—"keep silent, whatever may chance!"

She lay back on the couch, feigning slumber as Kane crossed the room and concealed himself behind some tapestries which, hanging upon the wall, hid a niche that might have once held a statue of some sort.

He had scarcely done so when the single door of the room opened and a strange barbaric figure stood framed in it. Nakari, queen of Negari, had come to her slave.

The woman was clad as she had been when he had seen her on the throne, and the colored armlets and anklets clanked as she closed the door behind her and came into the room. She moved with the easy sinuousness of a she-leopard and in spite of himself the watcher was struck with admiration for her lithe beauty. Yet at the same time a shudder of repulsion shook him, for her eyes gleamed with vibrant and magnetic evil, older than the world.

"Lilith!" thought Kane. "She is beautiful and terrible as Purgatory. She is Lilith—that foul, lovely woman of ancient legend."

Nakari halted by the couch, stood looking down upon her captive for a moment, then with an enigmatic smile, bent and shook her. Marylin opened her eyes, sat up, then slipped from her couch and knelt before her savage mistress—an act which caused Kane to curse beneath his breath. The queen laughed and seating herself upon the couch, motioned the girl to

rise, and then put an arm about her waist and drew
her upon her lap. Kane watched, puzzled, while
Nakari caressed the girl in a lazy, amused manner.
This might be affection, but to Kane it seemed more
like a sated leopard teasing its victim. There was an
air of mockery and studied cruelty about the whole
affair.

"You are very soft and pretty, Mara," Nakari murmured lazily, "much prettier than the other girls who
serve me. The time approaches, little one, for your
nuptial. And a fairer bride has never been borne up
the Black Stairs."

Marylin began to tremble and Kane thought she was
going to faint. Nakari's eyes gleamed strangely beneath her long-lashed drooping lids, and her full red
lips curved in a faint tantalizing smile. Her every
action seemed fraught with some sinister meaning.
Kane began to sweat profusely.

"Mara," said the queen, "you are honored above
all other girls, and yet you are not content. Think how
the girls of Negari will envy you, Mara, when the
priests sing the nuptial song and the Moon of Skulls
looks over the black crest of the Tower of Death.
Think, little bride-of-the-Master, how many girls have
given their lives to be his bride!"

And Nakari laughed in her hateful, musical way as
at a rare jest. And then suddenly she stopped short.
Her eyes narrowed to slits as they swept the room, and
her whole body tensed. Her hand went to her girdle
and came away with a long thin dagger. Kane sighted
along the barrel of his pistol, finger against the trigger.
Only a natural hesitancy against shooting a woman
kept him from sending death into the savage heart of
Nakari, for he believed that she was about to murder
the girl.

Then, with a lithe, cat-like motion, she thrust the
girl from her knees and bounded back across the room,
her eyes fixed with blazing intensity on the tapestry
behind which Kane stood. Had those keen eyes discovered him? He quickly learned.

"Who is there?" she rapped out fiercely. "Who hides behind those hangings? I do not see you nor hear you, but I know someone is there!"

Kane remained silent. Nakari's wild beast instinct had betrayed him, and he was uncertain as to what course to follow. His next actions depended on the queen.

"Mara!" Nakari's voice slashed like a whip, "who is behind those hangings? Answer me! Shall I give you a taste of the whip again?"

The girl seemed incapable of speech. She cowered where she had fallen, her beautiful eyes full of terror. Nakari, her blazing gaze never wavering, reached behind her with her free hand and gripped a cord hanging from the wall. She jerked viciously. Kane felt the tapestries whip back on either side of him and he stood revealed.

For a moment the strange tableau held—the gaunt adventurer in his blood-stained, tattered garments, the long pistol gripped in his right hand—across the room the savage queen in her barbaric finery, one arm still lifted to the cord, the other hand holding the dagger in front of her—the imprisoned girl cowering on the floor.

Then Kane spoke: "Keep silent, Nakari, or you die!"

The queen seemed numbed and struck speechless by the sudden apparition. Kane stepped from among the tapestries and slowly approached her.

"You!" she found her voice at last. "You must be he of whom the guardsmen spake! There are not two other white men in Negari! They said you fell to your death! How then—"

"Silence!" Kane's voice cut in harshly on her amazed babblings; he knew that the pistol meant nothing to her, but she sensed the threat of the long blade in his left hand. "Marylin," still unconsciously speaking in the river tribes' language, "take cords from the hangings and bind her—"

He was about the middle of the chamber now. Nakari's face had lost much of its helpless bewilderment and into her blazing eyes stole a crafty gleam. She deliberately let her dagger fall as in token of surrender, then suddenly her hands shot high above her head and gripped another thick cord. Kane heard Marylin scream, but before he could pull the trigger or even think, the floor fell beneath his feet and he shot down into abysmal blackness. He did not fall far and he landed on his feet; but the force of the fall sent him to his knees and even as he went down, sensing a presence in the darkness beside him, something crashed against his skull and he dropped into a yet blacker abyss of unconsciousness.

CHAPTER 4

DREAMS OF EMPIRE

Slowly Kane drifted back from the dim realms where the unseen assailant's bludgeon had hurled him. Something hindered the motion of his hands, and there was a metallic clanking when he sought to raise them to his aching, throbbing head.

He lay in utter darkness, but he could not determine whether this was absence of light, or whether he was still blinded by the blow. He dazedly collected his scattered faculties and realized that he was lying on a damp stone floor, shackled by wrist and ankle with heavy iron chains which were rough and rusty to the touch.

How long he lay there, he never knew. The silence was broken only by the drumming pulse in his own aching head and the scamper and chattering of rats. At last a red glow sprang up in the darkness and grew before his eyes. Framed in the grisly radiance rose the sinister and sardonic face of Nakari. Kane shook his head, striving to rid himself of the illusion. But the light grew and as his eyes accustomed themselves to it, he saw that it emanated from a torch borne in the hand of the queen.

In the illumination he now saw that he lay in a small dank cell whose walls, ceiling and floor were of stone. The heavy chains which held him captive were made fast to metal rings set deep in the wall. There was but one door, which was apparently of bronze.

Nakari set the torch in a niche near the door, and coming forward, stood over her captive, gazing down at him in a manner rather speculating than mocking.

"You are he who fought the men on the cliff." The remark was an assertion rather than a question. "They said you fell into the abyss—did they lie? Did you bribe them to lie? Or how did you escape? Are you a magician and did you fly to the bottom of the chasm and then fly to my palace? Speak!"

Kane remained silent. Nakari cursed.

"Speak or I will have your eyes torn out! I will cut your fingers off and burn your feet!"

She kicked him viciously, but Kane lay silent, his deep somber eyes boring up into her face, until the feral gleam faded from her eyes to be replaced by an avid interest and wonder.

She seated herself on a stone bench, resting her elbows on her knees and her chin on her hands.

"I never saw a white man before," she said. "Are all white men like you? Bah! That can not be! Most men are fools, black or white. I know that white men are not gods as the river tribes say—they are only men. I, who know all the ancient mysteries, say they are only men.

"But white men have strange mysteries too, they tell me—the wanderers of the river tribes and Mara. They have war clubs that make a noise like thunder and kill afar off—that thing which you held in your right hand, was that one of those clubs?"

Kane permitted himself a grim smile.

"Nakari, if you know all mysteries, how can I tell you aught that you know not already?"

"How deep and cold and strange your eyes are!" the queen said as if he had not spoken. "How strange your whole appearance is—and you have the bearing of a king! You do not fear me—I never met a man who neither loved nor feared me. You would never fear me, but you could learn to love me. Look at me, bold one—am I not beautiful?"

"You are beautiful," answered Kane.

Nakari smiled and then frowned. "The way you say that, it is no compliment. You hate me, do you not?"

"As a man hates a serpent," Kane replied bluntly.

Nakari's eyes blazed with almost insane fury. Her hands clenched until the long nails sank into the palms; then as quickly as her anger had arisen, it ebbed away.

"You have the heart of a king," she said calmly, "else you would fear me. Are you a king in your land?"

"I am only a landless wanderer."

"You might be a king here," Nakari said slowly.

Kane laughed grimly. "Do you offer me my life?"

"I offer you more than that!"

Kane's eyes narrowed as the queen leaned toward him, vibrant with suppressed excitement. "Kane, what is it that you want more than anything else in the world?"

"To take the white girl you call Mara, and go."

Nakari sank back with an impatient exclamation.

"You can not have her; she is the promised bride of the Master. Even I could not save her, even if I wished. Forget her. I will help you forget her. Listen, listen to the words of Nakari, queen of Negari! You say you are a landless man—I will make you a king! I will give you the world for a toy!

"No, no! Keep silent until I have finished," she rushed on, her words tumbling over each other in her eagerness. Her eyes blazed, her whole body quivered with dynamic intensity. "I have talked to travelers, to captives and slaves, men from far countries. I know that this land of mountains and rivers and jungle is not all the world. There are far-off nations and cities, and kings and queens to be crushed and broken.

"Negari is fading, her might is crumbling, but a

strong man beside her queen might build it up again
—might restore all her vanishing glory. Listen, Kane!
Sit by me on the throne of Negari! Send afar to your
people for the thunder-clubs to arm my warriors! My
nation is still lord of central Africa. Together we will
band the conquered tribes—call back the days when
the realm of ancient Negari spanned the land from sea
to sea! We will subjugate all the tribes of the river, the
plain and the sea-shore, and instead of slaying them
all, we will make one mighty army of them! And then,
when all Africa is under our heel, we will sweep forth
upon the world like a hungry lion to rend and tear and
destroy!"

Solomon's brain reeled. Perhaps it was the woman's
fierce magnetic personality, the dynamic power she
instilled in her fiery words, but at the moment her
wild plan seemed not at all wild and impossible. Lurid
and chaotic visions flamed through the Puritan's brain
—Europe torn by civil and religious strife, divided
against herself, betrayed by her rulers, tottering—aye,
Europe was in desperate straits now, and might prove
an easy victim for some strong savage race of conquerors. What man can say truthfully that in his heart
there lurks not a yearning for power and conquest?

For a moment the Devil sorely tempted Solomon
Kane. Then before his mind's eye rose the wistful, sad
face of Marylin Taferal, and Solomon cursed.

"Out on ye, daughter of Satan! Avaunt! Am I a
beast of the forest to lead your savage devils against
mine own people? Nay, no beast ever did so. Begone!
If you wish my friendship, set me free and let me go
with the girl."

Nakari leaped like a tiger-cat to her feet, her eyes
flaming now with passionate fury. A dagger gleamed
in her hand and she raised it high above Kane's breast
with a feline scream of hate. A moment she hovered
like a shadow of death above him; then her arm sank
and she laughed.

"Freedom? She will find her freedom when the
Moon of Skulls leers down on the Black Altar. As for

you, you shall rot in this dungeon. You are a fool; Africa's greatest queen has offered you her love and the empire of the world—and you revile her! You love the slave girl, perhaps? Until the Moon of Skulls she is mine and I leave you to think about this: that she shall be punished as I have punished her before— hung up by her wrists, naked, and whipped until she swoons!"

Nakari laughed as Kane tore savagely at his shackles. She crossed to the door, opened it, then hesitated and turned back for another word.

"This is a foul place, bold one, and maybe you hate me the more for chaining you here. Maybe in Nakari's beautiful throneroom, with wealth and luxury spread before you, you will look upon her with more favor. Very soon I shall send for you, but first I will leave you here awhile to reflect. Remember—love Nakari and the kingdom of the world is yours; hate her—this cell is your realm."

The bronze door clanged sullenly, but more hateful to the imprisoned Englishman was the venomous, silvery laugh of Nakari.

Time passed slowly in the darkness. After what seemed a long time the door opened again, this time to admit a huge warrior who brought food and a sort of thin wine. Kane ate and drank ravenously and afterward slept. The strain of the last few days had worn him greatly, mentally and physically, but when he awoke he felt fresh and strong.

Again the door opened and two great savage warriors entered. In the light of the torches they bore, Kane saw that they were giants, clad in loin-cloths and ostrich plume headgear, and bearing long spears in their hands.

"Nakari wishes you to come to her, white man," was all they said, as they took off his shackles. He arose, exultant in even brief freedom, his keen brain working fiercely for a way of escape.

Evidently the fame of his prowess had spread, for

the two warriors showed great respect for him. They
motioned him to precede them, and walked carefully
behind him, the points of their spears boring into his
back. Though they were two to one, and he was unarmed, they were taking no chances. The gazes they
directed at him were full of awe and suspicion.

Down a long, dark corridor they went, his captors
guiding him with light prods of their spears, up a
narrow winding stair, down another passageway, up
another stair, and then they emerged into the vast
maze of gigantic pillars into which Kane had first
come. As they started down this huge hall, Kane's eyes
suddenly fell on a strange and fantastic picture painted
on the wall ahead of him. His heart gave a sudden
leap as he recognized it. It was some distance in front
of him and he edged imperceptibly toward the wall
until he and his guards were walking along very close
to it. Now he was almost abreast of the picture and
could even make out the mark his dagger had made
upon it.

The warriors following Kane were amazed to hear
him gasp suddenly like a man struck by a spear. He
wavered in his stride and began clutching at the air
for support.

They eyed each other doubtfully and prodded him,
but he cried out like a dying man and slowly crumpled
to the floor, where he lay in a strange, unnatural position, one leg doubled back under him and one arm
half supporting his lolling body.

The guards looked at him fearfully. To all appear-
ances he was dying, but there was no wound upon
him. They threatened him with their spears, but he
paid no heed. Then they lowered their weapons uncertainly and one of them bent over him.

Then it happened. The instant the guard stooped
forward, Kane came up like a steel spring released.
His right fist following his motion curved up from his
hip in a whistling half-circle and crashed against the
warrior's jaw. Delivered with all the power of arm and
shoulder, propelled by the upthrust of the powerful

legs as Kane straightened, the blow was like that of a
slingshot. The guard slumped to the floor, unconscious
before his knees gave way.

The other warrior plunged forward with a bellow,
but even as his victim fell, Kane twisted aside and his
frantic hand found the secret spring in the painting
and pressed.

All happened in the breath of a second. Quick as
the warrior was, Kane was quicker, for he moved with
the dynamic speed of a famished wolf. For an instant
the falling body of the senseless guard hindered the
other warrior's thrust, and in that instant Kane felt
the hidden door give way. From the corner of his eye
he saw a long gleam of steel shooting for his heart.
He twisted about and hurled himself against the door,
vanishing through it even as the stabbing spear slit
the skin on his shoulder.

To the dazed and bewildered warrior, standing
there with weapon upraised for another thrust, it
seemed as if his prisoner had simply vanished through
a solid wall, for only a fantastic picture met his gaze
and this did not give to his efforts.

CHAPTER 5
"FOR A THOUSAND YEARS—"

Kane slammed the hidden door shut behind him,
jammed down the spring and for a moment leaned
against it, every muscle tensed, expecting to hold it
against the efforts of a horde of spearmen. But nothing
of the sort materialized. He heard his guard fumbling
outside for a time; then that sound, too, ceased. It
seemed impossible that these people should have lived
in this place as long as they had without discovering
the secret doors and passages, but it was a conclusion
which forced itself upon Kane's mind.

At last he decided that he was safe from pursuit for
the time being, and turning, started down the long,

narrow corridor with its eon-old dust and its dim gray light. He felt baffled and furious, though he was free from Nakari's shackles. He had no idea how long he had been in the palace; it seemed ages. It must be day now, for it was light in the outer halls, and he had seen no torches after they had left the subterranean dungeons.

He wondered if Nakari had carried out her threat of vengeance on the helpless girl, and swore passionately. Free for the time being, yes; but unarmed and hunted through this infernal palace like a rat. How could he aid either himself or Marylin? But his confidence never faltered. He was in the right and some way would present itself.

Suddenly a narrow stairway branched off the main passageway, and up this he went, the light growing stronger and stronger until he stood in the full glare of the African sunlight. The stair terminated in a sort of small landing directly in front of which was a tiny window, heavily barred. Through this he saw the blue sky tinted gold with the blazing sunlight. The sight was like wine to him and he drew in deep breaths of fresh, untainted air, breathing deep as if to rid his lungs of the aura of dust and decayed grandeur through which he had been passing.

He was looking out over a weird and bizarre landscape. Far to the right and the left loomed up great black crags and beneath them there reared castles and towers of stone, of strange architecture—it was as if giants from some other planet had thrown them up in a wild and chaotic debauch of creation. These buildings were backed solidly against the cliffs, and Kane knew that Nakari's palace also must be built into the wall of the crag behind it. He seemed to be in the front of that palace in a sort of minaret built on the outer wall. But there was only one window in it and his view was limited.

Far below him through the winding and narrow streets of that strange city, swarms of people went to and fro, seeming like black ants to the watcher above.

East, north and south, the cliffs formed a natural bulwark; only to the west was a built wall.

The sun was sinking west. Kane turned reluctantly from the barred window and went down the stairs again. Again he paced down the narrow gray corridor, aimlessly and planlessly, for what seemed miles and miles. He descended lower and lower into passages that lay below passages. The light grew dimmer, and a dank slime appeared on the walls. Then Kane halted, a faint sound from beyond the wall arresting him. What was that? A faint rattle—the rattle of chains.

Kane leaned close to the wall, and in the semi-darkness his hand encountered a rusty spring. He worked at it cautiously and presently felt the hidden door it betokened swing inward. He gazed out warily.

He was looking into a cell, the counterpart of the one in which he had been confined. A smoldering torch was thrust into a niche on the wall, and by its lurid and flickering light he made out a form on the floor, shackled wrist and ankle as he had been shackled.

A man; at first Kane thought him to be a native, but a second glance made him doubt. His skin was dark, but his features were finely chiseled, and he possessed a high, magnificent forehead, hard vibrant eyes, and straight dark hair.

The man spoke in an unfamiliar dialect, one which was strangely distinct and clear-cut in contrast to the guttural jargon of the natives with whom Kane was familiar. The Englishman spoke in English, and then in the language of the river tribes.

"You who come through the ancient door," said the other in the latter dialect, "who are you? You are no savage—at first I thought you one of the Old Race, but now I see you are not as they. Whence come you?"

"I am Solomon Kane," said the Puritan, "a prisoner in this devil-city. I come from far across the blue salt sea."

The man's eyes lighted at the word.

"The sea! The ancient and everlasting! The sea which I have never seen, but which cradled the glory of my ancestors! Tell me, stranger, have you, like they, sailed across the breast of the great blue monster, and have your eyes looked on the golden spires of Atlantis and the crimson walls of Mu?"

"Truly," answered Solomon uncertainly. "I have sailed the seas, even to Hindustan and Cathay, but of the countries you mention I know nothing."

"Nay," the other sighed. "I dream—I dream. Already the shadow of the great night falls across my brain and my words wander. Stranger, there have been times when these cold walls and floor have seemed to melt into green, surging deeps and my soul was filled with the deep booming of the everlasting sea. I who have never seen the sea!"

Kane shuddered involuntarily. Surely this man was insane. Suddenly the other shot out a withered, claw-like hand and gripped his arm, despite the hampering chain.

"You whose skin is so strangely fair! Have you seen Nakari, the she-fiend who rules this crumbling city?"

"I have seen her," said Kane grimly, "and now I flee like a hunted rat from her murderers."

"You hate her!" the other cried. "Ha, I know! You seek Mara, the white girl who is her slave?"

"Aye."

"Listen," the shackled one spoke with strange solemnity; "I am dying. Nakari's rack has done its work. I die and with me dies the shadow of the glory that was my nation's. For I am the last of my race. In all the world there is none like me. Hark now, to the voice of a dying race."

And Kane leaning there in the flickering semi-darkness of the cell heard the strangest tale to which man has ever listened, brought out of the mist of the dim dawn ages by the lips of delirium. Clear and distinct the words fell from the dying man and Kane alternately burned and froze as vista after gigantic vista of time and space swept up before him.

"Long eons ago—ages, ages ago—the empire of my race rose proudly above the waves. So long ago was it that no man remembers an ancestor who remembered it. In a great land to the west our cities rose. Our golden spires split the stars; our purple-prowed galleys broke the waves around the world, looting the sunset for its treasure and the sunrise for its wealth.

"Our legions swept forth to the north and to the south, to the west and the east, and none could stand before them. Our cities banded the world; we sent our colonies to all lands to subdue all savages, men of all colors, and enslave them. They toiled for us in the mines and at the galley's oars. All over the world the people of Atlantis reigned supreme. We were a sea-people, and we delved the deeps of all the oceans. The mysteries were known to us, and the secret things of land and sea and sky. We read the stars and were wise. Sons of the sea, we exalted him above all others.

"We worshipped Valka and Hotah, Honen and Golgor. Many virgins, many strong youths, died on their altars and the smoke of the shrines blotted out the sun. Then the sea rose and shook himself. He thundered from his abyss and the thrones of the world fell before him! New lands rose from the deep and Atlantis and Mu were swallowed up by the gulf. The green sea roared through the fanes and the castles, and the seaweed encrusted the golden spires and the topaz towers. The empire of Atlantis vanished and was forgotten, passing into the everlasting gulf of time and oblivion. Likewise the colony cities in barbaric lands, cut off from their mother kingdom, perished. The savage barbarians rose and burned and destroyed until in all the world only the colony city of Negari remained as a symbol of the lost empire.

"Here my ancestors ruled as kings, and the ancestors of Nakari—the she-cat!—bent the knee of slavery to them. Years passed, stretching into centuries. The empire of Negari dwindled. Tribe after tribe rose and flung off the chains, pressing the lines back from the sea, until at last the sons of Atlantis gave way entirely and retreated into the city itself—the last stronghold of the race. Conquerors no longer, hemmed in by ferocious tribes, yet they held those tribes at bay for a thousand years. Negari was invincible from without; her walls held firm; but within evil influences were at work.

"The sons of Atlantis had brought their slaves into the city with them. The rulers were warriors, scholars, priests, artisans; they did no menial work. For that they depended upon the slaves. There were more of these slaves than there were masters. And they increased while the sons of Atlantis dwindled.

"They mixed with each other more and more as the race degenerated until at last only the priestcraft was free of the taint of savage blood. Rulers sat on the throne of Negari who possessed little of the blood of Atlantis, and these allowed more and more wild tribesmen to enter the city in the guise of servants, mercenaries and friends.

"Then came a day when these fierce slaves revolted and slew all who bore a trace of the blood of Atlantis, except the priests and their families. These they imprisoned as 'fetish people.' For a thousand years savages have ruled in Negari, their kings guided by the captive priests, who though prisoners, were yet the masters of kings."

Kane listened enthralled. To his imaginative mind, the tale burned and lived with strange fire from cosmic time and space.

"After all the sons of Atlantis, save the priests, were dead, there rose a great king to the defiled throne of ancient Negari. He was a tiger and his warriors were like leopards. They called themselves Negari, ravishing even the name of their former masters, and none could stand before them. They swept the land from sea to sea, and the smoke of destruction put out the stars. The great river ran red and the new lords of Negari strode above the corpses of their tribal foes. Then the great king died and the empire crumbled, even as the Atlantean kingdom of Negari had crumbled.

"They were skilled in war. The dead sons of Atlantis, their former masters, had trained them well in the ways of battle, and against the wild tribesmen they were invincible. But only the ways of war had they learned, and the empire was torn with civil strife. Murder and intrigue stalked red-handed through the palaces and the streets, and the boundaries of the empire dwindled and dwindled. All the while, savage kings with red, frenzied brains sat on the throne, and behind the curtains, unseen but greatly feared, the Atlantean priests guided the nation, holding it together, keeping it from absolute destruction.

"Prisoners in the city were we, for there was nowhere else in the world to go. We moved like ghosts through the secret passages in the walls and under the earth, spying on intrigue and doing secret magic. We upheld the cause of the royal family—the descendants of that tiger-like king of long ago—against all plotting chiefs, and grim are the tales which these silent walls could tell.

"These savages are not like the other natives of the region. A latent insanity lurks in the brains of every one. They have tasted so deeply and so long of slaughter and victory that they are as human leopards, forever thirsting for blood. On their myriad wretched slaves they have sated all lusts and desires until they have become foul and terrible beasts, forever seeking some new sensation, forever quenching their fearful thirsts in blood.

"Like a lion have they lurked in these crags for a thousand years, to rush forth and ravage the jungle and river people, enslaving and destroying. They are still invincible from without, though their possessions have dwindled to the very walls of this city, and their former great conquests and invasions have dwindled to raids for slaves.

"But as they faded, so too faded their secret masters, the Atlantean priests. One by one they died, until only I remained. In the last century they too have mixed with their rulers and slaves, and now—oh, the shame upon me!—I, the last son of Atlantis, bear in my veins the taint of barbarian blood. They died; I remained, doing magic and guiding the savage kings, I the last priest of Negari. Then the she-fiend, Nakari, arose."

Kane leaned forward with quickened interest. New life surged into the tale as it touched upon his own time.

"Nakari!" the name was spat as a snake hisses; "slave and the daughter of a slave! Yet she prevailed when her hour came and all the royal family died.

"And me, the last son of Atlantis, me she prisoned and chained. She feared not the silent Atlantean priests, for she was the daughter of a Satellite—one of the lesser, native priests. They were men who did the menial work of the masters—performing the lesser sacrifices, divining from the livers of fowls and serpents and keeping the holy fires forever burning. Much she knew of us and our ways, and evil ambition burned in her.

"As a child she danced in the March of the New Moon, and as a young girl she was one of the Star-maidens. Much of the lesser mysteries was known to her, and more she learned, spying upon the secret rites of the priests who enacted hidden rituals that were old when the earth was young.

"For the remnants of Atlantis secretly kept alive the old worships of Valka and Hotah, Honen and Golgor, long forgotten and not to be understood by these savage people whose ancestors died screaming on their altars. Alone of all the savage Negari, she feared us not. Nakari not only overthrew the king and set herself on the throne, but she dominated the priests—the Satellites and the few Atlantean masters who were left. All these last, save me, died beneath the daggers of her assassins or on her racks. She alone of all the myriad savage thousands who have lived and died between these walls guessed at the hidden passages and subterranean corridors, secrets which we of the priest-craft had guarded jealously from the people for a thousand years.

"Ha! Ha! Blind, savage fools! To pass an ageless age in this city, yet never to learn of the secrets thereof! Apes—fools! Not even the lesser priests know of the long gray corridors, lit by phosphorescent ceilings, through which in bygone ages strange forms have glided silently. For our ancestors built Negari as they built Atlantis—on a mighty scale and with an unknown art. Not for men alone did we build, but for the gods who moved unseen among us. And deep the secrets these ancient walls hold!

"Torture could not wring these secrets from our lips, but shackled in her dungeons, we trod our hidden corridors no more. For years the dust has gathered there, untouched by human foot, while we, and finally I alone, lay chained in these foul cells. And among the temples and the dark, mysterious shrines of old, move vile Satellites, elevated by Nakari to glories that were once mine—for I am the last Atlantean high priest.

"Their doom is ascertained, and red will be their ruin! Valka and Golgor, gods lost and forgotten, whose memory shall die with me, strike down their walls and humble them unto the dust! Break the altars of their blind pagan gods—"

Kane realized that the man was wandering in his mind. The keen brain had begun to crumble at last.

"Tell me," said he; "you mentioned the fair girl, Mara. What do you know of her?"

"She was brought to Negari years ago by raiders," the other answered, "only a few years after the rise of the savage queen, whose slave she is. Little of her I know, for shortly after her arrival, Nakari turned on me—and the years that lie between have been grim dark years, shot red with torture and agony. Here I have lain, hampered by my chains from escape which lay in that door through which you entered—and for the knowledge of which Nakari has torn me on racks and suspended me over slow fires."

Kane shuddered. "You know not if they have so misused the white girl? Her eyes are haunted, and she has wasted away."

"She has danced with the Starmaidens at Nakari's command, and has looked on the bloody and terrible rites of the Black Temple. She has lived for years among a people with whom blood is cheaper than water, who delight in slaughter and foul torture, and such sights as she has looked upon would blast the eyes and wither the flesh of strong men. She has seen the victims of Nakura die amid horrid torments, and the sight is burned forever in the brain of the beholder. The rites of the Atlanteans the savages took whereby to honor their own crude gods, and though the essence of those rites is lost in the wasting years, yet even as Nakari's minions perform them, they are not such as men can look on, unshaken."

Kane was thinking: "A fair day for the world when this Atlantis sank, for most certainly it bred a race of strange and unknown evil." Aloud he said: "Who is this Master of whom Nakari spake, and what meant she by calling Mara his bride?"

"Nakura—Nakura. The skull of evil, the symbol of Death that they worship. What know these savages of the gods of sea-girt Atlantis? What know they of the dread and unseen gods whom their masters worshipped with majestic and mysterious rites? They understand not of the unseen essence, the invisible deity that reigns in the air and the elements; they must worship a material object, endowed with human shape. Nakura was the last great wizard of Atlantean Negari. A renegade he was, who conspired against his own people and aided the revolt of the savages. In life they followed him and in death they deified him. High in the Tower of Death his fleshless skull is set, and on that skull hinge the brains of all the people of Negari.

"Nay, we of Atlantis worshipped Death, but we likewise worshipped Life. These people worship only Death and call themselves Sons of Death. And the skull of Nakura has been to them for a thousand years the symbol of their power, the evidence of their greatness."

"Do you mean," Kane broke in impatiently on these ramblings, "that they will sacrifice the girl to their god?"

"In the Moon of Skulls she will die on the Black Altar."

"What in God's name is this Moon of Skulls?" Kane cried passionately.

"The full moon. At the full of each moon, which we name the Moon of Skulls, a virgin dies on the Black Altar before the Tower of Death, where centuries ago, virgins died in honor of Golgor, the god of Atlantis. Now from the face of the tower that once housed the glory of Golgor, leers down the skull of the renegade wizard, and the people believe that his brain still lives therein to guide the star of the city. For look ye, stranger, when the full moon gleams over the rim of the tower and the chant of the priests falls silent, then from the skull of Nakura thunders a great voice, raised in an ancient Atlantean chant, and the people fall on their faces before it.

"But hark, there is a secret way, a stair leading up to a hidden niche behind the skull, and there a priest lurks and chants. In days gone by one of the sons of Atlantis had this office, and by all rights of men and gods it should be mine this day. For though we sons of Atlantis worshipped our ancient gods in secret, these savages would have none of them. To hold our power we were devotees to their foul gods and we sang and sacrificed to him whose memory we cursed.

"But Nakari discovered the secret, known before only to the Atlantean priests, and now one of her Satellites mounts the hidden stair and yammers forth the strange and terrible chant which is but meaningless gibberish to him, as to those who hear it. I, and only I, know its grim and fearful meaning."

Kane's brain whirled in his efforts to formulate some plan of action. For the first time during the whole search for the girl, he felt himself against a blank wall. The palace was a labyrinth, a maze in which he could decide no direction. The corridors seemed to run without plan or purpose, and how could he find Marylin, prisoned as she doubtless was in one of the myriad chambers or cells? Or had she already passed over the borderline of life, or succumbed to the brutal torture-lust of Nakari?

He scarcely heard the ravings and mutterings of the dying man.

"Stranger, do you indeed live or are you but one of the ghosts which have haunted me of late, stealing through the darkness of my cell? Nay, you are flesh and blood—but you are a savage, even as Nakari's race are savages. Eons ago when your ancestors were defending their caves against the tiger and the mammoth, with crude spears of flint, the gold spires of my people split the stars! They are gone and forgotten, and the world is a waste of barbarians. Let me, too, pass as a dream that is forgotten in the mists of the ages—"

Kane rose and paced the cell. His fingers closed like steel talons as on a sword hilt and a blind red wave of fury surged through his brain. Oh God! to get his foes before the keen blade that had been taken from him—to face the whole city, one man against them all—

Kane pressed his hands against his temples.

"The moon was nearly full when last I saw it. But I know not how long ago that was. I know not how long I have been in this accursed palace, or how long I lay in that dungeon where Nakari threw me. The time of full moon may be past, and—oh merciful God!—Marylin may be dead already."

"Tonight is the Moon of Skulls," muttered the other; "I heard one of my jailers speak of it."

Kane gripped the dying man's shoulder with unconscious force.

"If you hate Nakari or love mankind, in God's name tell me how to save the child."

"Love mankind?" the priest laughed insanely. "What

has a son of Atlantis and a priest of forgotten Golgor to do with love? What are mortals but food for the jaws of the gods? Softer girls than your Mara have died screaming beneath these hands and my heart was as iron to their cries. Yet hate"—the strange eyes flamed with fearful light—"for hate I will tell you what you wish to know!

"Go to the Tower of Death when the moon is risen. Slay the false priest who lurks behind the skull of Nakura, and then when the chanting of the worshippers below ceases, and the masked slayer beside the Black Altar raises the sacrificial dagger, speak in a loud voice that the people can understand, bidding them set free the victim and offer up instead, Nakari, queen of Negari!

"As for the rest, afterward you must rely on your own craft and prowess if you come free."

Kane shook him.

"Swift! Tell me how I am to reach this tower!"

"Go back through the door whence you came." The man was sinking fast, his words dropped to whispers. "Turn to the left and go a hundred paces. Mount the stair you come to, as high as it goes. In the corridor where it ceases go straight for another hundred paces, and when you come to what seems a blank wall, feel over it until you find a projecting spring. Press this and enter the door which will open. You will then be out of the palace and in the cliffs against which it is built, and in the only one of the secret corridors known to the people of Negari. Turn to your right and go straight down the passage for five hundred paces. There you will come to a stair which leads up to the niche behind the skull. The Tower of Death is built into the cliff and projects above it. There are two stairs—"

Suddenly the voice trailed out. Kane leaned forward and shook the man, and the priest suddenly rose up with a great effort. His eyes blazed with a wild and unearthly light and he flung his shackled arms wide.

"The seal!" he cried in a great voice. "The golden

spires of Atlantis and the sun on the deep blue waters! I come!"

And as Kane reached to lay him down again, he slumped back, dead.

CHAPTER 6

THE SHATTERING OF THE SKULL

Kane wiped the cold sweat from his pale brow as he hurried down the shadowy passage. Outside this horrible palace it must be night. Even now the full moon —the grim Moon of Skulls—might be rising above the horizon. He paced off a hundred paces and came upon the stair the dying priest had mentioned.

This he mounted, and coming into the corridor above, he measured off another hundred paces and brought up short against what appeared to be a doorless wall. It seemed an age before his frantic fingers found a piece of projecting metal. There was a creak of rusty hinges as the hidden door swung open and Kane looked into a passageway darker than the one in which he stood.

He entered, and when the door shut behind him he turned to his right and groped his way along for five hundred paces. There the corridor was lighter; light sifted in from without, and Kane discerned a stairway. Up this he went for several steps, then halted, baffled. At a sort of landing the stairway became two, one leading away to the left, the other to the right. Kane cursed. He felt that he could not afford to make a mistake—time was too precious—but how was he to know which would lead him to the niche where the priest hid?

The Atlantean had been about to tell him of these stairs when struck by the delirium which precedes death, and Kane wished fervently that he had lived only a few moments longer.

At any rate, he had no time to waste; right or wrong,

he must chance it. He chose the right-hand stair and ran swiftly up it. No time for caution now.

He felt instinctively that the time of sacrifice was close at hand. He came into another passage and discerned by the change in masonry that he was out of the cliffs again and in some building—presumably the Tower of Death. He expected any moment to come upon another stair, and suddenly his expectations were realized—but instead of up, it led down. From somewhere in front of him Kane heard a vague, rhythmic murmur and a cold hand gripped his heart. The chanting of the worshippers before the Black Altar!

He raced forward recklessly, rounded a turn in the corridor, brought up short against a door and looked through a tiny aperture. His heart sank. He had chosen the wrong stair and had wandered into some other building adjoining the Tower of Death.

He looked upon a grim and terrible scene. In a wide open space before a great black tower whose spire rose above the crags behind it, two long lines of savage dancers swayed and writhed. Their voices rose in a strange meaningless chant, and they did not move from their tracks.

From their knees upward their bodies swayed in fantastic rhythmical motions, and in their hands torches tossed and whirled, shedding a lurid shifting red light over the scene. Behind them were ranged a vast concourse of people who stood silent.

The dancing torchlight gleamed on a sea of glittering eyes and eager faces. In front of the dancers rose the Tower of Death, gigantically tall, black and horrific. No door or window opened in its face, but high on the wall in a sort of ornamented frame there leered a grim symbol of death and decay. The skull of Nakura! A faint, eery glow surrounded it, lit somehow from within the tower, Kane knew, and wondered by what strange art the priests had kept the skull from decay and dissolution so long.

But it was neither the skull nor the tower which gripped the Puritan's horrified gaze and held it. Be-

tween the converging lines of yelling, swaying worshippers there rose a great black altar. On this altar lay
a slim, white shape.

"Marylin!" the word burst from Kane's lips in a
great sob.

For a moment he stood frozen, helpless, struck
blind. No time now to retrace his steps and find the
niche where the skull priest lurked.

Even now a faint glow was apparent behind the
spire of the tower, etching that spire blackly against
the sky. The moon had risen. The chant of the dancers
soared up to a frenzy of sound, and from the silent
watchers behind them began a sinister low rumble of
drums. To Kane's dazed mind it seemed that he looked
on some red debauch of a lower Hell.

What ghastly worship of past eons did these per-
verted and degenerate rites symbolize? Kane knew
that these people aped the rituals of their former
masters in their crude way, and even in his despair
he found time to shudder at the thought of what those
original rites must have been.

Now a fearful shape rose up beside the altar
where lay the silent girl. A tall figure, entirely naked
save for a hideous painted mask on his face and a
great headdress of waving plumes. The drone of the
chant sank low for an instant, then rose up again to
wilder heights. Was it the vibrations of their song that
made the floor quiver beneath Kane's feet?

Kane with shaking fingers began to unbar the door.
Naught to do now but to rush out barehanded and die
beside the girl he could not save. Then his gaze was
blocked by a giant form which shouldered in front of
the door. A huge man, a chief by his bearing and
apparel, leaned idly against the wall as he watched
the proceedings. Kane's heart gave a great leap. This
was too good to be true! Thrust in the chief's girdle
was the pistol that he himself had carried! He knew
that his weapons must have been divided among his
captors. This pistol meant nothing to the chief, but he
must have been taken by its strange shape and was

carrying it as savages will wear useless trinkets. Or
perhaps he thought it a sort of war-club. At any rate,
there it was. And again floor and building seemed to
tremble.

Kane pulled the door silently inward and crouched
in the shadows behind his victim like a great brooding
tiger.

His brain worked swiftly and formulated his plan
of action. There was a dagger in the girdle beside the
pistol; the chief's back was turned squarely to him and
he must strike from the left to reach the heart and
silence him quickly. All this passed through Solomon's
brain in a flash as he crouched.

The chief was not aware of his foe's presence until
Kane's lean right hand shot across his shoulder and
clamped on his mouth, jerking him backward. At the
same instant the Puritan's left hand tore the dagger
from the girdle and with one desperate plunge sank
the keen blade home.

The warrior crumpled without a sound and in an
instant Kane's pistol was in its owner's hand. A second's investigation showed that it was still loaded and
the flint still in place.

No one had seen the swift murder. Those few who
stood near the doorway were all facing the Black
Altar, enwrapped in the drama which was there un-
folding. As Kane stepped across the corpse, the chanting of the dancers ceased abruptly. In the instant of
silence which followed, Kane heard, above the pounding of his own pulse, the nightwind rustle the death-
like plumes of the masked horror beside the altar. A
rim of the moon glowed above the spire.

Then, from high up on the face of the Tower of
Death, a deep voice boomed out in a strange chant.
Mayhap the priest who spoke behind the skull knew
not what his words meant, but Kane believed that he
at least mimicked the very intonation of those long-
dead Atlantean acolytes. Deep, mystic, resonant the
voice sounded out, like the endless flowing of long
tides on the broad white beaches.

The masked one beside the altar drew himself up to his great height and raised a long, glimmering blade. Kane recognized his own sword, even as he leveled his pistol and fired—not at the masked priest but full at the skull which gleamed in the face of the tower. For in one blinding flash of intuition he remembered the dying Atlantean's words: "Their brains hinge on the skull of Nakura!"

Simultaneously with the crack of the pistol came a shattering crash; the dry skull flew into a thousand pieces and vanished, and behind it the chant broke off short in a death shriek. The rapier fell from the hand of the masked priest and many of the dancers crumpled to the earth, the others halting short, spellbound. Through the deathly silence which reigned for an instant, Kane rushed toward the altar; then all Hell broke loose.

A babel of bestial screams rose to the shuddering stars. For centuries only their faith in the dead Nakura had held together the blood-drenched brains of the savage Negari. Now their symbol had vanished, had been blasted into nothing before their eyes. It was to them as if the skies had split, the moon fallen and the world ended. All the red visions which lurked at the backs of their corroded brains leaped into fearful life, all the latent insanity which was their heritage rose to claim its own, and Kane looked upon a whole nation turned to bellowing maniacs.

Screaming and roaring they turned on each other, men and women, tearing with frenzied fingernails, stabbing with spears and daggers, beating each other with the flaming torches, while over all rose the roar of frantic human beasts.

With clubbed pistol Kane battered his way through the surging, writhing ocean of flesh, to the foot of the altar stairs. Nails raked him, knives slashed at him, torches scorched his garments, but he paid no heed.

Then as he reached the altar, a terrible figure broke from the struggling mass and charged him. Nakari, queen of Negari, crazed as any of her subjects, rushed

upon the Englishman with dagger bared and eyes
horribly aflame.

"You shall not escape this time!" she was screaming,
but before she reached him a great warrior, dripping
blood and blind from a gash across his eyes, reeled
across her path and lurched into her.

She screamed like a wounded cat and struck her
dagger into him, and then groping hands closed on
her. The blind giant whirled her on high with one
dying effort, and her last scream knifed the din of
battle as Nakari, last queen of Negari, crashed against
the stones of the altar and fell shattered and dead at
Kane's feet.

Kane sprang up the black steps, worn deep by the
feet of myriad priests and victims, and as he came,
the masked figure, who had stood like one turned to
stone, came suddenly to life. He bent swiftly, caught
up the sword he had dropped and thrust savagely at
the charging Englishman. But the dynamic quickness
of Solomon Kane was such as few men could match.
A twist and sway of his steely body and he was inside
the thrust, and as the blade slid harmlessly between
arm and chest, he brought down the heavy pistol
barrel among the waving plumes, crushing headdress,
mask and skull with one blow.

Then ere he turned to the fainting girl who lay
bound on the altar, he flung aside the shattered pistol
and snatched his stolen sword from the nerveless hand
which still grasped it, feeling a fierce thrill of renewed
confidence at the familiar feel of the hilt.

Marylin lay white and silent, her death-like face
turned blindly to the light of the moon which shone
calmly down on the frenzied scene. At first Kane
thought her to be dead, but his searching fingers
detected a faint flutter of pulse.

He cut her bonds and lifted her tenderly—only to
drop her again and whirl as a hideous, blood-stained
figure of insanity came leaping and gibbering up the
steps. Full upon Kane's out-thrust blade the creature

ran, and toppled back into the red swirl below, clawing beast-like at its mortal wound.

Then beneath Kane's feet the altar rocked; a sudden tremor hurled him to his knees and his horrified eyes beheld the Tower of Death sway to and fro.

Some horror of Nature was taking place, and this fact pierced the crumbling brains of the fiends who fought and screamed below. A new element entered into their shrieking, and then the Tower of Death swayed far out with a terrible and awesome majesty —broke from the rocking crags and gave way with a thunder of crashing worlds. Great stones and shards of masonry came raining down, bringing death and destruction to hundreds of screaming humans below.

One of these stones crashed to pieces on the altar beside Kane, showering him with dust.

"Earthquake!" he gasped, and smitten by this new terror he caught up the senseless girl and plunged recklessly down the cracking steps, hacking and stabbing a way through the crimson whirlpools of bestial humanity that still tore and ravened.

The rest was a red nightmare in which Kane's dazed brain refused to record all its horrors. It seemed that for screaming crimson centuries he reeled through narrow winding streets where bellowing, screeching demons battled and died, among titanic walls and black columns that rocked against the sky and crashed to ruin about him, while the earth heaved and trembled beneath his staggering feet and the thunder of crashing towers filled the world.

Gibbering fiends in human shape clutched and clawed at him, to fade before his flailing sword, and falling stones bruised and battered him. He crouched as he reeled along, covering the girl with his body as best he could, sheltering her alike from blind stone and blinder human.

At last, when it seemed mortal endurance had reached its limit, he saw the great black outer wall of the city loom before him, rent from earth to parapet and tottering for its fall. He dashed through a crevice, and gathering his efforts, made one last sprint. And scarce was he out of reach than the wall crashed, falling inward like a great black wave.

The night wind was in his face and behind him rose the clamor of the doomed city as Kane staggered down the hill path that trembled beneath his feet.

CHAPTER 7
THE FAITH OF SOLOMON

Dawn lay like a cool white hand on the brow of Solomon Kane. The nightmares faded from his soul as he breathed deep of the morning wind which blew up from the jungle far below his feet—a wind laden with the musk of decaying vegetation. Yet it was like the breath of life to him, for the scents were those of the clean natural disintegration of outdoor things, not the loathsome aura of decadent antiquity that lurks in the walls of eon-old cities—Kane shuddered involuntarily.

He bent over the sleeping girl who lay at his feet, arranged as comfortably as possible with the few soft tree branches he had been able to find for her bed. Now she opened her eyes and stared about wildly for an instant; then as her gaze met the face of Solomon, lighted by one of his rare smiles, she gave a little sob of thankfulness and clung to him.

"Oh, Captain Kane! Have we in truth escaped from yon fearful city? Now it seems all like a dream—after you fell through the secret door in my chamber Nakari later went to your dungeon—as she told me—and returned in vile humor. She said you were a fool, for she had offered you the kingdom of the world and you had but insulted her. She screamed and raved and cursed like one insane and swore that she would yet, alone, build a great empire of Negari.

"Then she turned on me and reviled me, saying that you held me—a slave—in more esteem than a queen and all her glory. And in spite of my pleas she took me across her knees and whipped me until I swooned.

"Afterward I lay half senseless for a long time, and was only dimly aware that men came to Nakari and said that you had escaped. They said you were a sorcerer, for you faded through a solid wall like a ghost. But Nakari killed the men who had brought you from the cell, and for hours she was like a wild beast.

"How long I lay thus I know not. In those terrible rooms and corridors where no natural sunlight ever entered, one lost all track of time. But from the time you were captured by Nakari and the time that I was placed on the altar, at least a day and a night and another day must have passed. It was only a few hours before the sacrifice that word came you had escaped.

"Nakari and her Starmaidens came to prepare me for the rite." At the bare memory of that fearful ordeal she whimpered and hid her face in her hands. "I must have been drugged—I only know that they clothed me in the white robe of the sacrifice and carried me into a great black chamber filled with horrid statues.

"There I lay for a space like one in a trance, while the women performed various strange and shameful rites according to their grim religion. Then I fell into a swoon, and when I emerged I was lying bound on the Black Altar—the torches were tossing and the devotees chanting—behind the Tower of Death the rising moon was beginning to glow—all this I knew faintly, as in a deep dream. And as in a dream I saw the glowing skull high on the tower—and the gaunt, naked priest holding a sword above my heart; then I knew no more. What happened?"

"At about that moment," Kane answered, "I emerged from a building wherein I had wandered by mistake, and blasted their hellish skull to atoms with a pistol ball. Whereupon, all these people, being cursed from birth by demons, and being likewise possessed of devils, fell to slaying one another. In the midst of the tumult an earthquake cometh to pass which shakes the walls down. Then I snatch you up, and running at random, come upon a rent in the outer wall and thereby escape, carrying you, who seem in a swoon.

"Once only you awoke, after I had crossed the Bridge-Across-the-Sky, as the people of Negari called it, which was crumbling beneath our feet by reason of the earthquake. After I had come to these cliffs, but dared not descend them in the darkness, the moon being nigh to setting by that time, you awoke and screamed and clung to me, whereupon I soothed you as best I might, and after a time you fell into a natural sleep."

"And now what?" asked the girl.

"England!" Kane's deep eyes lighted at the word. "I find it hard to remain in the land of my birth for more than a month at a time; yet though I am cursed with the wanderlust, 'tis a name which ever rouses a glow in my bosom. And how of you, child?"

"Oh heaven!" she cried, clasping her small hands. "Home! Something of which to be dreamed—never attained, I fear. Oh Captain Kane, how shall we gain through all the vast leagues of jungle which lie between this place and the coast?"

"Marylin," said Kane gently, stroking her curly hair, "methinks you lack somewhat in faith, both in Providence and in me. Nay, alone I am a weak creature, having no strength or might in me; yet in times past hath God made me a great vessel of wrath and a sword of deliverance. And, I trust, shall do so again.

"Look you, little Marylin: in the last few hours as it were, we have seen the passing of an evil race and the fall of a foul empire. Men died by thousands about us, and the earth rose beneath our feet, hurling down towers that broke the heavens; yea, death fell about us in a red rain, yet we escaped unscathed.

"Therein is more than the hand of man! Nay, a Power—the mightiest Power! That which guided me across the world, straight to that demon city—which led me to your chamber—which aided me to escape again and led me to the one man in all the city who would give the information I must have, the strange, evil priest of an elder race who lay dying in a subterranean cell—and which guided me to the outer wall, as I ran blindly and at random—for should I have come under the cliffs which formed the rest of the wall, we had surely perished. That same Power brought us safely out of the dying city, and safe across the rocking bridge—which shattered and thundered down into the chasm just as my feet touched solid earth!

"Think you that having led me this far, and accomplished such wonders, the Power will strike us down now? Nay! Evil flourishes and rules in the cities of men and the waste places of the world, but anon the great giant that is God rises and smites for the righteous, and they lay faith on him.

"I say this: this cliff shall we descend in safety, and yon dank jungle traverse in safety, and it is as sure that in old Devon your people shall clasp you again to their bosom, as that you stand here."

And now for the first time Marylin smiled, with the quick eagerness of a normal young girl, and Kane sighed in relief. Already the ghosts were fading from her haunted eyes, and Kane looked to the day when her horrible experiences should be as a dimming dream. One glance he flung behind him, where beyond the scowling hills the lost city of Negari lay shattered and silent, amid the ruins of her own walls and the fallen crags which had kept her invincible so long, but which had at last betrayed her to her doom.

A momentary pang smote him as he thought of the myriad of crushed, still forms lying amid those ruins; then the blasting memory of their evil crimes surged over him and his eyes hardened.

"And it shall come to pass, that he who fleeth from the noise of the fear shall fall into the pit; and he that cometh up out of the midst of the pit shall be taken in the snare; for the windows from on high are open, and the foundations of the earth do shake.

"For Thou hast made of a city an heap; of a de-

fended city a ruin; a palace of strangers to be no city;
it shall never be built.

"Moreover, the multitude of Thy strangers shall be
like small dust and the multitude of the terrible ones
shall be as chaff that passeth suddenly away; yea, it
shall be at an instant suddenly.

"Stay yourselves and wonder; cry ye out and cry;
they are drunken but not with wine; they stagger but
not with strong drink.

"Verily, Marylin," said Kane with a sigh, "with
mine own eyes have I seen the prophecies of Isaiah
come to pass. They were drunken but not with wine!
Nay, blood was their drink and in that red flood they
dipped deep and terribly."

Then taking the girl by the hand he started toward
the edge of the cliff. At this very point had he
ascended in the night—how long ago it seemed.

Kane's clothing hung in tatters about him. He was
torn, scratched and bruised. But in his eyes shone the
clear calm light of serenity as the sun came up, flooding cliffs and jungle with a golden light that was like
a promise of joy and happiness.

THE ONE BLACK STAIN

Sir Thomas Doughty, executed at St. Julian's Bay, 1578

They carried him out on the barren sand where the
 rebel captains died;
Where the grim gray rotting gibbets stand as Magellan
 reared them on the strand,
And the gulls that haunt the lonesome land wail to the
 lonely tide.

Drake faced them all like a lion at bay, with his lion
 head upflung:
"Dare ye my word of law defy, to say that this traitor
 shall not die?"
And his captains dared not meet his eye but each man
 held his tongue.

Solomon Kane stood forth alone, grim man of a somber
 race:
"Worthy of death he well may be, but the court ye
 held was a mockery,
"Ye hid your spite in a travesty where Justice hid her
 face.

"More of the man had ye been, on deck your sword to
 cleanly draw
"In forthright fury from its sheath, and openly cleave
 him to the teeth—
"Rather than slink and hide beneath a hollow word
 of Law."

Hell rose in the eyes of Francis Drake. "Puritan knave!"
 swore he,

"Headsman, give him the axe instead! He shall strike
    off yon traitor's head!"
Solomon folded his arms and said, darkly and
    somberly:

"I am no slave for your butcher's work." "Bind him
    with triple strands!"
Drake roared in wrath and the men obeyed, hesitantly,
    as men afraid,
But Kane moved not as they took his blade and
    pinioned his iron hands.

They bent the doomed man to his knees, the man who
    was to die;
They saw his lips in a strange smile bend; one last
    long look they saw him send
At Drake, his judge and his one-time friend, who dared
    not meet his eye.

The axe flashed silver in the sun, a red arch slashed
    the sand;
A voice cried out as the head fell clear, and the
    watchers flinched in sudden fear,
Though 'twas but a sea-bird wheeling near above the
    lonely strand.

"This be every traitor's end!" Drake cried, and yet
    again;
Slowly his captains turned and went, and the admiral's
    stare was elsewhere bent
Than where cold scorn with anger blent in the eyes of
    Solomon Kane.

Night fell on the crawling waves; the admiral's door
    was closed;
Solomon lay in the stenching hole; his irons clashed as
    the ship rolled.
And his guard, grown weary and overbold, laid down
    his pike and dozed.

He woke with a hand at his corded throat that gripped
    him like a vise;

*Trembling, he yielded up the key, and the somber
      Puritan stood up free,*
*His cold eyes gleaming murderously with the wrath
      that is slow to rise.*

*Unseen, to the admiral's cabin door went Solomon
      from the guard,*
*Through the night and silence of the ship, the guard's
      keen dagger in his grip;*
*No man of the dull crew saw him slip in through the
      door unbarred.*

Drake at the table sat alone, his face sunk in his hands;
*He looked up, as from sleeping—but his eyes were
      blank with weeping*
*As if he saw not, creeping, Death's swiftly flowing
      sands.*

*He reached no hand for gun or blade to halt the hand
      of Kane,*
*Nor even seemed to hear or see, lost in black mists
      of memory,*
*Love turned to hate and treachery, and bitter, canker-
      ing pain.*

*A moment Solomon Kane stood there, the dagger
      poised before,*
*As a condor stoops above a bird, and Francis Drake
      spoke not nor stirred,*
*And Kane went forth without a word and closed the
      cabin door.*

BLADES OF THE BROTHERHOOD

"Death is a blue flame dancing over corpses"
—Solomon Kane

CHAPTER 1
SWORDS CLASH AND A STRANGER COMES

The blades crossed with a vicious clash of steel; blue sparks showered. Across those blades hot eyes burned into each other—hard black eyes and volcanic blue ones. Breath hissed between locked teeth; feet scruffed the sward, advancing, retreating.

He of the black eyes feinted and thrust as quick as a snake strikes. The blue-eyed youth parried with a half turn of a steely wrist and his counter stroke was like the flash of summer lightning.

"Hold, gentlemen!" The swords were struck up and a portly man stood between the combatants, jeweled rapier in one hand, cocked hat in the other.

"Have done! The matter is decided and honor satisfied! Sir George is wounded!"

The black-eyed man with an impatient gesture put behind him his left arm from which blood was streaming.

"Stand aside!" cried he furiously and with an oath, "a wound—a scratch! It decides nothing! 'Tis no matter. This must be to the death!"

"Aye, stand aside, Sir Rupert," said the victor, quietly, but his blue eyes were sparks of steel, "the matter between us can be settled only by death!"

"Put up your steel, you young cockerels!" snapped Sir Rupert. "As magistrate I command it! Sir physician, come and look to Sir George's wound. Jack Hollinster, sheathe your blade, sirrah! I'll have no bloody murders in this district an' my name be Rupert d'Arcy."

Young Hollinster said nothing, nor did he obey the choleric magistrate's command, but he dropped his sword point to the earth and with head half lowered, stood silent and moody, watching the company from under frowning black brows.

Sir George had hesitated, but one of his seconds whispered urgently in his ear and he sullenly acquiesced, handed his sword to the speaker and gave himself up to the ministrations of the physician.

It was a bleak setting for such a scene. A low level land, sparsely grown with sickly grass, now withered, ran to a wide strip of white sand, strewn with bits of driftwood. Beyond the sand the sea washed gray and restless, a dead thing upon whose desolate bosom the only sign of life was a single sail hovering in the distance. Inland, across the bleak moors there could be seen in the distance the drab cottages of a small village.

In such a barren and desolate landscape, the splash of color and passionate life there on the beach contrasted strangely. The pale autumn sun flashed on the bright blades, the jeweled hilts, the silver buttons on the coats of some of the men, and the gilt-work on Sir Rupert's cocked hat.

Sir George's seconds were helping him in his coat, and Hollinster's second, a sturdy young man in homespun, was urging him to don his. But Jack, still resentful, put him aside. Suddenly he sprang forward with his sword still in his hand and spoke, his voice ringing fierce and vibrant with passion.

"Sir George Banway, look to yourself! A scratch in the arm will not blot out the insult whereof you know! The next time we meet there will be no magistrate to save your rotten hide!"

The nobleman whirled round with a black oath, and

Sir Rupert started forward with a roar: "Sirrah! How dare you—"

Hollinster snarled in his face and turning his back, strode away, sheathing his sword with a vicious thrust. Sir George made as if to follow him, his dark face contorted, but his friend whispered again in his ear, motioning seaward. Banway's eyes wandered to the single sail which hung as if suspended in the sky and he nodded grimly.

Hollinster strode along the beach in silence, bare-headed, hat in one hand and his coat slung over his arm. The chill wind brought coolness to his sweat-plastered locks, but not to his turmoiled brain.

His second, Randel, followed him in silence. As they progressed along the beach, the scenery became more wild and rugged; gigantic rocks, gray and moss-grown, reared their heads along the shore and straggled out to meet the waves in grim jagged lines. Further out a dangerous reef sent up a low and continuous moaning.

Jack Hollinster stopped, turned his face seaward and cursed long, fervently and deep-throatedly. The awed listener understood the burden of his profanity to be regret at the fact that he, Hollinster, had failed to sink his blade to the hilt in the black heart of that swine, that jackal, that damned rogue, Sir George Banway!

"And now," he snarled, "it's like the villain will never meet me in fair combat again, having tasted my steel, but by God—"

"Calm yourself, Jack," honest Randel squirmed uneasily; he was Hollinster's closest friend but he did not understand the black furious moods into which his comrade sometimes fell. "You drubbed him fairly; he got the worst o' it all around. After all, you'd hardly kill a man for what he did—"

"No?" Jack cried passionately, "I'd hardly kill a man for that foul insult? Well, not a man, but a base rogue of a nobleman whose heart I'll see before the moon wanes! Do you realize that he publicly slandered Mary

Garvin, the girl I love? That he befouled her name
over his drinking cup in the tavern? Why—"

"That I understand," sighed Randel, "having heard
the full details not less than a score of times. Also I
know that you threw a cup of wine in his face, slapped
his chops, upset a table on him and kicked him twice
or thrice. Troth, Jack, you've done enough for any
man! Sir George is highly connected—you are but the
son of a retired sea-captain—even though you have
distinguished yourself for valor abroad. Well, after all
Jack, Sir George need not have fought you at all. He
might have claimed his rank and had his serving men
flog you forth."

"An' he had," Hollinster said grimly with a vicious
snap of his teeth, "I had put a pistol ball between
his damned black eyes—Dick, leave me to my folly.
You preach the right road I know—the path of for-
bearance and meekness. But I have lived where a
man's only guide and aid was the sword at his belt;
and I come of hot wild blood. Just now that blood
is stirred to the marrow by reason of that swine-
nobleman. He knew Mary was my beloved, yet he sat
there and insulted her in my presence—aye, in my
very teeth! with a leer at me. And why? Because he
has monies, lands, titles—high family connections and
noble blood. I am a poor man and a poor man's son,
who carries his fortune in a sheath at the belt-side.
Had I, or had Mary been of high birth, he had re-
spected—"

"Pshaw!" broke in Randel. "When did George Banway ever respect—anything? His black name hereabouts is well deserved. He respects his own desires."

"And he desires Mary," moodily growled the other.
"Well, mayhap he'll take her as he's taken many
another maid hereabouts. But first he'll kill John Hollinster. Dick—I would not appear churlish but mayhap you'd better leave me for a space. I am no fit
companion to anyone and I need solitude and the cold
breath of the sea to cool my burning blood."

"You'll not seek Sir George——" Randel hesitated.

Jack made a gesture of impatience. "I'll go the other way, I promise you. Sir George went home to coddle his scratch. He'll not show his face for a fortnight."

"But Jack, his bullies are of unsavory repute. Is it safe for you?"

Jack grinned wolfishly.

"Never fear; if he strikes back *that* way—'twill be in the darkness of night—not in open day."

Randel walked away toward the village, shaking his head dubiously, and Jack strode on along the beach, each step taking him further away from the habitations of man and further into a dim realm of waste lands and waste waters. The wind sighed through his clothing, cutting like a knife, but he did not don his coat. The cold gray aura of the day lay like a shroud over his soul and he cursed the land and the clime.

His soul hungered for the far warm southern lands he had known in his wanderings, but a face rose in his visions—a laughing girlish face crowned with golden curls, in whose eyes lay a warmth which transcended the golden heat of tropic moons and which rendered even this barren country warm and pleasant.

Then in his musings another face rose—a dark mocking face, with hard black eyes and a cruel mouth curled viciously under a thin black mustache. Jack Hollinster cursed sincerely.

A deep vibrant voice broke in on his profanity.

"Young man, your words are as sounding brass and tinkling cymbals, full of sound and fury, signifying nothing."

Jack whirled, hand at hilt. On a great gray boulder there sat a stranger. This man rose as Jack turned, unwrapping a wide black cloak and laying it over his arm.

Hollinster gazed at him curiously. The man was of a type to command attention and something more.

He was inches taller than Hollinster who was considerably above medium height. There was no ounce of fat or surplus flesh on that spare frame, yet the man did not look frail or even too thin. On the contrary. His broad shoulders, deep chest and long rangy limbs betokened strength, speed and endurance—bespoke the swordsman as plainly as did the long unadorned rapier at his belt. The man reminded Jack, more than anything else, of one of the gaunt gray wolves he had seen on the Siberian steppes.

But it was the face which first caught and held the young man's attention. The face was rather long, smooth-shaven and of a strange dark pallor which together with the somewhat sunken cheeks lent an almost corpse-like appearance at times—until one looked at the eyes. These gleamed with vibrant life and dynamic vitality, pent deep and ironly controlled. Looking directly into these eyes, feeling the cold shock of their strange power, Jack Hollinster was unable to tell their color. There was the grayness of ancient ice in them, but there was also the cold blueness of the Northern sea's deepest depths. Heavy black brows hung above them and the whole effect of the countenance was distinctly Mephistophelean.

The stranger's cloth was severely plain and suited the man. His hat was a black slouch, featherless. From heel to neck he was clad in close-fitting garments of a somber hue, unrelieved by an ornament or jewel. No ring adorned his powerful fingers; no gem twinkled on his rapier hilt and its long blade was cased in a plain leather sheath. There were no silver buttons on his garments, no bright buckles on his shoes.

Strangely enough the drab monotone of his dress was broken in a novel and bizarre manner by a wide sash knotted gypsy-fashion about his waist. This sash was silk of Oriental workmanship; its color was a shimmering green, and from it projected a dirk hilt and the butts of two heavy pistols.

Hollinster's gaze wandered over this strange apparition even as he wondered how this man came here, in his strange apparel, armed to the teeth. His appearance suggested the Puritan, yet—

"How come you here?" asked Jack bluntly. "And how is it that I saw you not until you spoke?"

"I came here as all honest men come, young sir," the deep voice answered, as the speaker wrapped his wide black cloak about him and reseated himself on the boulder, "on my two legs—as for the other: men engrossed in their own affairs to the point of taking the Name in vain, see neither their friends—to their shame—nor their foes—to their harm."

"Who are you?"

"My name is Solomon Kane, young sir, a landless man—one time of Devon."

Jack frowned uncertainly. Somewhere, somehow, the Puritan had certainly lost all the unmistakable Devonshire accent. From the sound of his words he might have been from anywhere in England, north or south.

"You have travelled a great deal, sir?"

"My steps have been led in many far countries, young sir."

A light broke in on Hollinster and he gazed at his strange companion with quickened interest.

"Were you not a captain in the French army for a space, and were you not at—" he named a certain name.

Kane's brow clouded.

"Aye. I led a rout of ungodly men, to my shame be it said, though the cause was a just one. In the sack of that town you name, many foul deeds were done under the cloak of the cause and my heart was sickened—oh, well—many a tide has flowed under the bridge since then, and I have drowned some red memories in the sea—

"And speaking of the sea, lad, what make you of yonder ship standing off and on as she hath done since yesterday's daybreak?"

A lean finger stabbed seaward, and Jack shook his head.

"She lies too far out. I can make naught of her."

The somber eyes bored into his and Hollinster did not doubt that that cold gaze might plumb the distances and detect the very name painted on the far away ship's bows. Anything seemed possible for those strange eyes.

"'Tis in truth a thought far for the eye to carry," said Kane, "but by the cut of her rigging I believe I recognize her. It is in my mind that I would like to meet the master of this ship."

Jack said nothing. There was no harbor hereabouts, but a ship might, in calm weather, run close ashore and anchor just outside the reef. This ship might be a smuggler. There was always a good deal of illicit trade going on about this lonely coast where the custom officers seldom came.

"Have you ever heard of one Jonas Hardraker, whom men call the Fishhawk?"

Hollinster started. That dread name was known on all the coasts of the civilized world, and in many uncivilized coasts, for the owner had made it feared and abhorred in many waters, warm and cold. Jack sought to read the stranger's face, but the brooding eyes were inscrutable.

"That bloody pirate? The last I heard of him, he was purported to be cruising the Caribees."

Kane nodded.

"Lies travel ahead of a fast craft. The Fishhawk cruises where his ship is, and where his ship is, only his master Satan knows."

He stood up, wrapping his cloak more closely about him.

"The Lord hath led my feet into many strange places, and over many queer paths," said he somberly. "Some were fair and many were foul; sometimes I seemed to wander without purpose or guidance but always when I sought deep I found fit reason therefor.

And harkee, lad, forbye the fires of Hell there is no
hotter fire than the blue flame of vengeance which
burneth a man's heart night and day without rest until
he quench it in blood.

"It hath been my duty in times past to ease various
evil men of their lives—well, the Lord is my staff and
my guide and methinks he hath delivered mine enemy
into mine hands."

And so saying Kane strode away with long cat-like
strides, leaving Hollinster to gape after him in bewilderment.

CHAPTER 2

ONE COMES IN THE NIGHT

Jack Hollinster awoke from a dream-haunted slumber. He sat up in bed and stared about him. Outside
the moon had not risen but in his window a head and
a pair of broad shoulders were framed black in the
starlight. A warning "Shhhh!" came to him like a
serpent's hiss.

Slipping his sword from the scabbard which hung
on the bed post, Jack rose and approached the window. A bearded face set with two small sparkling
eyes looked in at him; the man was breathing deeply
as if from a long run.

"Bring tha swoord, lad, and follow me," came the
urgent whisper. "'E's got she!"

"How now? Who's got who?"

"Sir Garge!" was the chilling whisper. "'E sent she
a writin' wi' your name onto it, biddin' 'er come to the
Rocks, and his rogues grabbed she and—"

"Mary Garvin?"

"Truth as ever was, maaster!"

The room reeled. Hollinster had anticipated attack
on himself; he had not supposed the villainy of Sir
George's nature went deep enough for an abduction
of a helpless girl.

"Blast his black soul," he growled between his teeth as he snatched at his clothes. "Where is she now?"

"They tooken she to 'is 'ouse, sur."

"And who are you?"

"No' but poor Sam as tends stable down to the tavern, sur. I see 'em grab she."

Dressed and bare sword in hand, Hollinster climbed through the window.

"I thank you, Sam," said he. "If I live, I'll remember this."

Sam grinned, showing his yellow fangs: "I'll go wi' 'e, maaster; I've a grudge or twain to settle wi' Sir Gargel!" He flourished a wicked bludgeon.

"Come then. We'll go straight to the swine's house."

Sir George Banway's ancient manor house, in which he lived alone except for a few evil-visaged servants and several more evil cronies, stood two miles from the village, close to the beach but in the opposite direction from that taken by Jack in his stroll yesterday. A great lowering hulk of a house, in some disrepair, its oaken panels stained with age, many ill tales were told about it, and of the villagers, only such rowdies and ruffians as enjoyed the owner's confidence, had ever set foot in it. No wall surrounded it, only ragged hedges and a few straggling trees. The moors ran to the back of the house and the front faced a strip of sandy beach some two hundred yards wide which lay between the house and the boulder-torn surf. The rocks directly in front of the house, at the water's edge were unusually high, barren and rugged. It was said that there were curious caves among them, but no one knew exactly for Sir George regarded that particular strip of beach as his own private property and had a way of taking musket shots at parties who showed a curiosity regarding it.

Not a light showed in the house as Jack Hollinster and his strange follower made their way across the dank moor. A thin mist had blotted out most of the stars and through it the great black house reared up dark and ominous, surrounded by dark, bent ghosts which were hedges and trees. Seaward, all was veiled in a gray shroud but once Jack thought he heard the muffled clank of a mooring chain. He wondered if a ship could be anchored outside that venomous line of breakers. The gray sea moaned restlessly as a sleeping monster might moan without waking.

"The windy, sur," came from Sam in a fierce whisper. "'E'll have the glims doused but 'e be there, just the same!"

Together they stole silently to the great dark house. Jack found time to wonder at the apparent lack of guards. Was Sir George so certain of himself that he had not taken the trouble to throw out sentries? Or were the sentries sleeping on duty? He tried a window cautiously. It was heavily shuttered but the shutters swung open with surprising ease. Even as they did, a suspicion crossed his mind like a lightning flash—all this was too easy! He whirled, just in time to see the bludgeon in Sam's hand descending. There was no time to thrust or duck. Yet even in that fleeting flash of vision he saw the triumph in the little glittering eyes—then the world crashed about him and all was utter blackness.

CHAPTER 3

"DEATH'S WALKIN' TONIGHT"

Slowly Jack Hollinster drifted back to consciousness. A red glow was in his eyes and he blinked repeatedly. His head ached sickeningly and this glare hurt his eyes. He shut them, hoping it would cease, but the merciless radiance beat through the lids—into his throbbing brain, it seemed. A confused medley of voices bore dimly on his ears. He tried to raise his hand to his head but was unable to stir. Then it all came back with a rush and he was fully and poignantly awake.

He was bound hand and foot and was lying on a dank dirt floor. He was in a vast cellar, piled high with squat casks and kegs and black sticky-looking barrels. The roof of this cellar was fairly high, braced with heavy oaken timbers. On one of these timbers hung a lanthorn from which emanated the glow that hurt his eyes. This light illuminated the cellar but filled its corners with flickering shadows. A flight of broad stone stairs came down the cellar at one end and a dark passageway led away out of the other end.

There were many men in the cellar; Jack recognized the dark mocking countenance of Banway, the drink-flushed face of the traitor Sam, two or three bullies who divided their time between Sir George's house and the village tavern. The rest, some ten or twelve men, he did not know. They were all indubitably sea-men; brawny hairy men with ear rings and nose rings and tarry breeches. But their dress was bizarre and grotesque. Some had gay bandannas bound about their heads and all were armed to the teeth. Cutlasses with broad brass guards were much in evidence as well as jewel-hilted daggers and silver-chased pistols. These men diced and drank and swore terrific oaths, while their eyes gleamed terribly in the lanthorn light.

Pirates! No true honest seamen, these, with their strange contrast of finery and ruffianism. Tarry breeks and seamen's shirts, yet silken sashes lapped their waists; no stockings to their legs, yet many had on silver-buckled shoes and heavy gold rings to their fingers. Great gems dangled from many a heavy gold hoop serving as ear ring. Not an honest sailorman's knife among them, but costly Spanish and Italian daggers. Their gauds, their ferocious faces, their wild and blasphemous bearing stamped them with the mark of their red trade.

Jack thought of the ship he had seen before sun-down and of the rattle of the anchor chain in the mist. He suddenly remembered the strange man, Kane, and wondered at his words. Had he known that ship was a buccaneer? What was his connection with these wild men? Was his Puritanism merely a mask to hide sinister activities?

A man casting dice with Sir George turned suddenly toward the captive. A tall, rangy, broad-shouldered man—Jack's heart leaped into his mouth. Then subsided. At first glimpse he had thought this man to be Kane, but he now saw that the buccaneer, though alike to the Puritan in general build, was his antithesis in all other ways. He was scantily but gaudily clad, and ornate with silken sash, silver buckles and gilded tassels. His broad girdle bristled with dagger hilts and pistol butts, scintillant with jewels. A long rapier, resplendent with gold-work and gems, hung from a rich scroll-worked baldric. From each slim gold ear ring was pendant a sparkling red ruby whose crimson brilliance contrasted strangely with the dark face.

This face was lean, hawk-like and cruel. A cocked hat topped the narrow high forehead, pulled low over sparse black brows, but not too low to hide the gay bandanna beneath. In the shadow of the hat a pair of cold gray eyes danced recklessly, with changing sparks of light and shadow. A knife-bridged beak of a nose hooked over a thin gash of a mouth, and the cruel upper lips were adorned with long drooping mustachios, much like those worn by Manchu mandarins.

"Ho, George, our guest wakes!" this man shouted with a cruel slash of laughter in his words. "By Zeus, Sam, I'd thought you'd given him his resting dose. But he'd a thicker pate than I thought for."

The pirate crew ceased their games and stared curiously or mockingly at Jack. Sir George's face darkened and he indicated his left arm, with the bandage showing through the ruffled silk sleeve.

"You spoke truth, Hollinster, when you said with our next meeting no magistrate should intervene. Only now, methinks 'tis *your* rotten hide shall suffer."

"*Jack!*"

Deeper than Banway's taunts, the sudden agonized voice cut like a knife. Jack, with his blood turning to ice, wrenched frantically over and craning his neck, saw a sight that almost stopped his heart. A girl was bound to a great ring in an oaken support—a girl who knelt on the dank dirt floor, straining toward him, her face white, her eyes dilated with fright, her golden locks in disarray—

"Mary—oh my God!" burst from Jack's anguished lips. A brutal shout of laughter chorused his frantic outcry.

"Drink a health to the loving pair!" roared the tall pirate captain, lifting a frothing drinking jack. "Drink to the lovers, lads! Meseemeth he grudges us our company. Wouldst be alone with the little wench, boy?"

"You black-hearted swine!" raved Jack, struggling to his knees with a superhuman effort. "You cowards, you poltroons, you dastards, you white-livered devils! Gods of Hell, if my arms were but free! Loose me, an' the pack of you have a drop of manhood between you all! Loose me, and let me at your swine-throats with my bare hands! If I make not corpses of jackals, then blast me for a varlet and a coward!"

"Judas!" spoke one of the buccaneers admiringly. "The lad hath the good right guts, even so! And what a flow o' speech, keelhaul me! Blast my lights and liver, cap'n, but—"

"Be silent," cut in Sir George harshly, for his hatred ate at his heart like a rat. "Hollinster, you waste your breath. Not this time do I face you with naked blade. You had your chance and failed. This time I fight you with weapons better suited to your rank and station. None knows where you went or to what end. None shall ever know. The sea has hidden better bodies than yours, and shall hide still better ones after your bones have turned to slime on the sea bottom. As for you—" he turned to the horrified girl who was stammering pitiful pleas, "you will bide with me awhile in my house. In this very cellar, belike. Then when I have wearied of you—"

"Hadst better be wearied of her by the time I return, in two months," broke in the pirate captain with a sort of fiendish joviality. "If I take a corpse to sea this trip—which Satan knoweth is a plaguey evil cargo!—I must have a fairer passenger next time."

Sir George grinned sourly. "So be it. In two months she is yours—unless she should chance to die before that time. You sail just before dawn with the red ruin of a man I intend to make of Hollinster wrapped in canvas, and you sink the remains so far out at sea they will never wash ashore. That is understood—then in two months you may return for the girl."

As Jack listened to this frightful program his heart shrivelled within him.

"Mary, my girl," he said weakly, "how came you here?"

"A man brought a missive," she whispered, too faint with fear to speak aloud. "It was written in a hand much like yours, with your name signed. It said that you were hurt and for me to come to you to the Rocks. I came; these men seized me and bore me here through a long tunnel."

"As I told 'e, maaster!" shouted the hirsute Sam with gloating glee. "Trust ole Sam to trick 'em! 'E come along same as a lamb! Oh, that were a rare trick—and a rare fool 'e were, too!"

"Belay," spoke up a dark, lean saturnine pirate, evidently first mate, "'tis perilous enough puttin' in this way to get rid o' the loot we takes. What if they find the girl here and she tips 'em the lay? Where'd we find a market this side the Channel for the North Sea plunder?"

Sir George and the captain laughed.

"Be at ease, Allardine. Wast ever a melancholy knave. They'll think the wench and the lad eloped together. Her father is against him, George says. None of the villagers will ever see or hear of either of them again and they'll never look here. You're downhearted because we're so far from the Main. Faith man, haven't we threaded the Channel before, aye, and taken merchantmen in the Baltic, under the very noses of the men-o'-war?"

"Mayhap," mumbled Allardine, "but I'll feel safer wi' these waters far behind. The day o' the Brotherhood is passin' in these climes. Best the Caribs for us. I feel evil in my bones. Death hovers over us like a black cloud and I see no channel to steer through."

The pirates moved uneasily. "Avast man, that's ill talk."

"It's an ill bed, the sea bottom," answered the other gloomily.

"Cheer up," laughed the captain, slapping his despondent mate resoundingly on the back. "Drink a swig o' rum to the bride! It's a foul berth, Execution Dock, but we're well to windward of *that*, so far. Drink to the bride! Ha ha! George's bride and mine—though the little hussy seems not overjoyful—"

"Hold!" the mate's head jerked up. "Was not that a muffled scream overhead?"

Silence fell while eyes rolled toward the stair and thumbs stealthily felt the edge of blades. The captain shrugged his mighty shoulders impatiently.

"I heard nothing."

"I did. A scream and a fallin' carcass—I tell you, Death's walkin' tonight—"

"Allardine," said the captain, with a sort of still passion as he knocked the neck from a bottle, "you are become an old woman, in very truth of late, starting at shadows. Take heart from me! Do I ever fret myself wi' fear or worry?"

"Better if you went wi' more heed," answered the gloomy one direly. "A-takin' o' break-neck chances, night and day—and wi' a human wolf on your trail day and night as you have—ha' you forgot the word sent you near two years ago?"

"Bah!" the captain laughed, raising the bottle to his lips. "The trail's too long for even—"

A black shadow fell across him and the bottle slipped from his fingers to shatter on the floor. As if struck by a premonition, the pirate paled and turned slowly. All eyes sought the stone stairway which led down into the cellar. No one had heard a door open or shut, but there on the steps stood a tall man, dressed all in black save for a bright green sash about his waist. Under heavy black brows, shadowed by a low-drawn slouch hat, two cold eyes gleamed like burning ice. Each hand gripped a heavy pistol, cocked. Solomon Kane!

CHAPTER 4

THE QUENCHING OF THE FLAME

"Move not, Jonas Hardraker," said Kane tonelessly. "Stir not, Ben Allardine! George Banway, John Harker, Black Mike, Bristol Tom—keep your hands in front of you! Let no man touch sword or pistol, lest he die suddenly!"

There were nearly twenty men in that cellar, but in those black muzzles there was sure death for two, and none wished to be the first to die. So nobody moved. Only the mate Allardine with his face like snow on a winding sheet, gasped:

"Kane! I knew it! Death's in the air when he's near! I told you, near two years ago when he sent you word, Jonas, and you laughed! I told you he came like a shadow and slew like a ghost! The red Indians in the new lands are naught to him in subtlety! Oh, Jonas, you should ha' harkened to me!"

Kane's somber eyes chilled him into silence. "You remember me of old, Ben Allardine—you knew me before the brotherhood of buccaneers turned into a bloody gang of cutthroat pirates. And I had dealings with your former captain, as we both remember—in the Tortugas and again off the Horn. An evil man he was and one whom Hell fire hath no doubt devoured —to which end I aided him with a musket ball.

"As to my subtlety—true I have dwelt in Darien and learned somewhat of stealth and woodcraft and strategy, but your true pirate is a very ox and easy to steal upon. Those who watch outside the house saw me not as I stole through the thick fog, and the bold rover who with sword and musket guarded the cellar door, knew not that I entered the house; he died suddenly and with only a short squeal like a stuck hog."

Hardraker burst out with a furious oath: "What do you here?"

Solomon Kane regarded him with a stare that was blood-chilling in its bleak certitude of doom.

"Some of your crew know me of old, Jonas Hardraker whom men call the Fishhawk," Kane's voice was toneless but deep feeling hummed at the back of it, "and you well know why I have followed you from the Main to Portugal, from Portugal to England. Two years ago you sank a ship in the Caribbees, *The Flying Heart* out of Dover. Thereon was a young girl, the daughter of—well, never mind the name. You remember the girl. The old man, her father, was a close friend to me, and many a time, in bygone years have I held his infant daughter on my knee—the infant who grew up to be torn by your foul hands, you bloody dog. Well, when the ship was taken, this maid fell into your clutches and shortly died. Death was more kind to her than you had been. Her father who learned of her fate from survivors of that massacre, went mad and is in such state to this day. She had no brothers, no one but that old man. None might avenge her—"

"Except you, Sir Galahad?" sneered the Fishhawk.

"Yes, I, you damned bloody swine!" roared Kane unexpectedly. The crash of his powerful voice almost shattered the ear drums and hardened buccaneers started and blenched. Nothing is more stunning or terrible than the sight of a man of icy nerves and iron control suddenly losing that control and flaming into a full withering blast of murderous fury. For a fleeting instant as he thundered those words, Kane was a fearful picture of primitive, incarnate passion. Then the storm passed instantly and he was himself again— cold as chill steel, deadly as a cobra.

One black muzzle centered on Hardraker's breast, the other menaced the rest of the gang.

"Make your peace with God, pirate," said Kane tonelessly, "for in another instant it will be too late."

Now for the first time the pirate blenched.

"Great God," he gasped, sweat beading his brow, "you'd not shoot me down like a jackal, without a chance?"

"That will I, Jonas Hardraker," answered Kane, with never a tremor of voice or steely hand, "and with a joyful heart. Have you not committed all crimes under the sun? Are you not a stench in the nostrils of God and a black smirch on the books of men? Have you ever spared weakness or pitied helplessness? Shrink you from your fate, you poor coward?"

With a terrific effort the pirate pulled himself together.

"Why, I shrink not. But it is *you* who are the coward."

Menace and added fury clouded the cold eyes for an instant. Kane seemed to retreat within himself—to withdraw himself still further from human contact. He poised himself there on the stairs like some brooding unhuman thing—like a great black condor about to rend and slay.

"You are a coward," continued the pirate recklessly, realizing—for he was no fool—that he had touched the one weak spot in Kane's armor—vanity. Though he never boasted, Kane took a deep pride in the fact that whatever his many enemies said of him, no man had ever called him a coward.

"Mayhap I deserve killing in cold blood," went on the Fishhawk, watching him narrowly, "but if you give me no chance to defend myself, men will name you poltroon."

"The praise or the blame of man is vanity," said

Kane somberly. "And men know if I be coward or not."

"But not I!" shouted Hardraker triumphantly. "An' you shoot me down I will go into Eternity, knowing you are a dastard, despite what men say or think of you!"

After all, Kane, fanatic as he was, was still human. He tried to make himself believe that he cared not what this wretch said or thought, but in his heart he knew that so deep was his underlying vanity of courage, that if this pirate died with a scornful sneer on his lips, that he, Kane, would feel the sting all the rest of his life. He nodded grimly.

"So be it. You shall have your chance, though the Lord knoweth you deserve naught. Name your weapons."

The Fishhawk's eyes narrowed. Kane's skill with the sword was a byword among the wild outcasts and rovers that wandered over the world. With pistols, he, Hardraker, would have no opportunity for trickery or to use his iron strength.

"Knives!" he snapped with a vicious snap of his strong white teeth.

Kane eyed him moodily for a moment, the pistols never wavering, then a faint grim smile spread over his dark countenance.

"Good enough; knives are scarce a gentleman's arm —but with one an end may be made which is neither quick nor painless."

He turned to the pirates. "Throw down your weapons." Sullenly they obeyed.

"Now loose the girl and the youth." This also was done and Jack stretched his numbed limbs, felt the cut in his head, now clotted with dried blood, and took the whimpering Mary in his arms.

"Let the girl go," he whispered, but Solomon shook his head.

"She could never get by the guards outside the house."

Kane motioned Jack to stand part way up the stairs, with Mary behind him. He gave Hollinster the pistols and swiftly undid his sword belt and jacket, laying them on the lower step. Hardraker was laying aside his various weapons and stripping to his breeches.

"Watch them all," Kane muttered. "I'll take care of the Fishhawk. If any other reaches for a weapon, shoot quick and straight. If I fall, flee up the stairs with the girl. But my brain is afire with the blue flame of vengeance and I will not fall!"

The two men now approached each other, Kane bareheaded and in his shirt, Hardraker still wearing his knotted bandanna, but stripped to the waist. The pirate was armed with a long Turkish dagger which he held point upward. Kane held a dirk in front of him as a man holds a rapier. Experienced fighters, neither held his blade point down in the conventional manner—which is unscientific and awkward, except in special cases.

It was a strange, nightmare scene that was lighted by the guttering lanthorn on the wall: the pale youth with his pistols on the stair with the shrinking girl behind him, the fierce hairy faces ringed about the walls, eyes glittering with savage intensity—the gleam on the dull blue blades—the tall figures in the center circling each other while their shadows kept pace with their movements, changing and shifting as they advanced or gave ground.

"Come in and fight, Puritan," taunted the pirate, yet giving ground before Kane's steady though wary approach. "Think of the wench, Broadbrim!"

"I *am* thinking of her, offal of Purgatory," said Kane somberly. "There be many fires, scum, some hotter than others—" how deadly blue the blades shimmered in the lanthorn light!—"but, save the fires of Hell—all fires—may be quenched—by—*blood!*"

And Kane struck as a wolf leaps. Hardraker parried the straight thrust and springing in, struck upward.

Kane's down-turned point deflected the sweep of the blade and with a dynamic coil and release of steel-spring muscles, the pirate bounded backward out of reach. Kane came on in a relentless surge; he was ever the aggressor in any battle. He thrust like lightning for face and body and for an instant the pirate was too busy parrying the whistling strokes to launch an attack of his own. This could not last; a knife fight is necessarily short and deadly. The nature of the weapons prevents any long drawn play of fencing skill.

Now Hardraker, watching his opportunity, suddenly caught Kane's knife wrist in an iron grip and at the same time ripped savagely for the belly. Kane, at the cost of a badly cut hand, caught the uplunging wrist and checked the point an inch from his body. There for a moment they stood like statues glaring into each other's eyes, exerting all their strength.

Kane did not care for this style of fighting. He had rather trust the other way which was more swiftly deadly—the open free style, the leaping in and out, thrusting and parrying, where one relied on his quickness of hand and foot and eye, and gave and invited open strokes. But since it was to be a test of strength— so be it!

Hardraker had already begun to doubt. Never had he met a man his equal in sheer brute power, but now he found this Puritan as immovable as iron. He threw all his strength, which was immense, into his wrists and his powerfully braced legs. Kane had shifted his grip on his dirk to suit the emergency. At first grips, Hardraker had forced Kane's knife hand upward. Now Solomon held his dirk poised above the pirate's breast, point downward. His task at hand was to force down the hand that gripped his wrist until he could drive the dirk through Hardraker's breast. The Fishhawk's knife hand was held low, the blade upward; he sought to strain against Kane's arresting left hand and braced arm until he could rip open the Puritan's belly.

So there they strained, man to man, until the muscles bulged in tortured knots all over them and sweat stood out on their foreheads. The veins swelled in Hardraker's temples. In the watching ring breath hissed sharply between clenched teeth.

For awhile neither gained the advantage. Then slowly but surely, Kane began to force Hardraker backwards. The locked hands of the men did not change in their relative position but the pirate's whole body began to sway. The pirate's thin lips split in a ghastly grin of superhuman effort, in which there was no mirth. His face was like a grinning skull and the eyes bulged from their sockets. Inflexibly as Death, Kane's greater strength asserted itself. The Fishhawk bent slowly like a tree whose roots are ripped up and which falls slowly. His breath hissed and whistled as he fought fiercely to brace himself like steel, to regain his lost ground. But back and down he went, inch by inch, until after what seemed hours, his back was pressed hard against an oaken table top and Kane loomed over him like a harbinger of Doom.

Hardraker's right hand still gripped his dagger, his left hand was still locked on Kane's right wrist. But now Kane, holding the dagger point still at bay with his left, began to force his knife hand downward. The veins stood out on Kane's temples with the effort. Inch by inch, as he had forced the Fishhawk down on the table, he forced the dirk downward. The muscles coiled and swelled like tortured steel cables in the pirate's slowly bending left arm, but slowly the dirk descended. Sometimes the Fishhawk managed to halt its relentless course for an instant, but he could never force it back by a fraction of an inch. He wrenched desperately with his right hand which still gripped the Turkish dagger, but Kane's bloody left hand held it as in a steel vise.

Now the implacable dirk point was within an inch of the pirate's heaving breast, and Kane's deathly cold eyes matched the chill of the blue steel. Within two inches of that evil heart the point stopped, held fixed by the desperation of the doomed man. What were those distended eyes seeing? There was a faraway glassy stare in them, though they were focussed on the dirk point which was the center of the universe to them. But what else did they see?—Sinking ships that the black sea drank and gurgled over? Coastal towns lit with red flame, where women screamed and through whose red glow dark figures leaped and blasphemed? Black seas, wild with winds and lit with the sheet lightning of an outraged heaven? Smoke and flame and red ruin—black shapes dangling at the yard-arms—writhing figures that fell from a plank laid out over the rail—a white girlish shape whose pallid lips framed frenzied pleas—?

From Hardraker's slavering lips burst a terrible scream. Kane's hand lurched downward—the dirk point sank into the breast. On the stairs Mary Garvin turned away, pressed her face against the dank wall to shut out sight—covered her ears to shut out sound.

Hardraker had dropped his dagger; he sought to tear loose his right hand to fend off that cruel dirk. But Kane held him, vise-like. Yet still the writhing pirate did not release Kane's wrist. Holding death at bay to the bitter end, he clutched and as Kane had forced the point to his breast, so he forced it into his heart—inch by inch. The sight brought cold sweat to the brows of the onlookers, but Kane's icy eyes never flickered. He too was thinking of a bloodstained deck and a weak young girl who cried in vain for mercy.

Hardraker's screams rose unbearably, thinned to a frightful thin squealing; not the cries of a coward afraid of the dark, but the blind unconscious howling of a man in his death agony. The hilt of the dirk almost touched his breast when the screaming broke in a ghastly strangled gurgling and then ceased. Blood burst from the ashy lips and the wrist in Kane's left hand went limp. Only then did the fingers of the left hand fall away from Kane's knife wrist—relaxed by the death they had striven so madly to hold at bay.

Silence lay like a white shroud over all. Kane wrenched his dirk clear and a trickle of seeping blood followed sluggishly, then ceased. The Puritan mechanically swished the blade through the air to shake off the red drops which clung to the steel, and as it flashed in the lanthorn light, it seemed to Jack Hollinster to glitter like a blue flame—a flame which had been quenched in scarlet.

Kane reached for his rapier. At that instant, Hollinster, jerking himself out of his trance-like mood, saw the man Sam stealthily lift a pistol and aim at the Puritan. Sight and action were as one. At the crash of Jack's shot Sam screamed and reared upright, his pistol exploding in the air. He had been crouched directly under the lanthorn. As he flung out his arms in his death throes, the pistol barrel struck the lanthorn and shattered it, plunging the cellar into instant blackness.

Instantly the darkness crashed into sound, strident and blasphemous. Kegs were upset, men fell over each other and swore soulfully, steel clashed and pistols cracked as men found them with groping hands and fired at random. Somebody howled profanely as one of these blind bullets found a mark. Jack had the girl by the arm and was half leading, half carrying her up the dark stairs. He slipped and stumbled, but eventually reached the top and flung open the heavy door. A faint light which this opening let in showed him a man just behind him and a dim flood of figures scrambling up the lower steps.

Hollinster swung the remaining loaded pistol around, then Kane's voice spoke:

" 'Tis I—Kane—young sir. Out swiftly, with your lady."

Hollinster obeyed and Kane, leaping out after him, turned and slammed the oaken door in the faces of the yelling horde which surged up from below. He dropped a strong bolt into place and then stepped back. Inside sounded muffled yells, hammerings and shots, and in places the wood of the door bulged outward as bullets chunked into the other side. But none of the soft lead went entirely through the thick hard panels.

"And now what?" asked Jack turning to the tall Puritan. He noticed for the first time that a bizarre figure lay at his feet—a dead pirate with ear rings and gay sash, whose sword and musket lay beside him. Undoubtedly the sentry whose watch Kane's silent sword had ended.

The Puritan casually shoved the corpse aside with his foot and motioned the two lovers to follow him. He led the way up a short flight of wooden steps, down a dark hallway, into a chamber, then halted. The chamber was lit by a large candle on a table.

"Wait here a moment," he requested. "Most of the evil ones are confined below, but there be guards without—some five or six men. I slipped between them as I came, but now the moon is out and we must be wary. I will look through an outer window and see if I can spy any."

Left alone in the chamber, Jack looked at Mary in love and pity. This had been a hectic night for any girl. And Mary, poor child, had never been used to violence and ill treatment. Her face was so pale that Jack wondered if the color would ever come back into her once rosy cheeks. Her eyes were wide and haunted, though trusting when she looked at her lover.

He drew her gently into his arms. "Mary girl—" he began tenderly when, looking over his shoulder, she screamed, her eyes flaring with new terror. Instantaneously came the scrape of a rusty bolt.

Hollinster whirled. A black opening gaped in the wall where formerly had been only one of the regular panels. Before it stood Sir George Banway, eyes blazing, garments dishevelled, pistols leveled.

Jack flung Mary aside and threw up his weapon.

The two shots crashed together. Hollinster felt the bullet cut the skin on his cheek like a red-hot razor edge. A bit of cloth flew from Sir George's shirt bosom. With a sobbing gasp of curse he went down—then as Jack turned back to the horrified girl, Banway reeled up again. He was drinking in the air in great gasps as if his breath had been driven out of him, but he did not seem hurt and there was no spot of blood about him.

Aghast and astounded—for he knew the ball had struck squarely—Jack stood gaping, holding the smoking pistol, until Sir George knocked him sprawling with a hard buffet of his fist. Then Hollinster bounded up, raging, but in that second Banway snatched the girl, and dragging her in a brutal grip, leaped back through the opening with her, slamming shut the secret panel. Solomon Kane, returning as fast as his long legs could carry him, found Hollinster raving and bruising his bare fists against a blank wall.

A few gasping words interlarded with wild blasphemies and burning self-reproaches, gave Kane the situation.

"The hand of Satan is over him," raved the frantic youth. "Full in the breast I shot him—yet he took no hurt! Oh, fool and drooling imbecile I am—I stood there like an image instead of rushing him with the barrel for a club—stood there like a blind, dumb fool while he—"

"Fool that I am, not to have thought that this house might have secret passages," said the Puritan. "Of course this secret doorway leads into the cellar. But stay—" as Hollinster would have attacked the panel with the dead sailor's cutlass which Kane had brought. "Even if we open the secret door and go into the cellar that way, or back through the bolted stair-door, they will shoot us like rabbits, uselessly. Now be calm for a moment, and harken:

"You saw that dark passageway leading out of the cellar? Well, it is in my mind that there must be a tunnel which leads to the rocks along the sea shore.

Banway has long been in league with smugglers and pirates. Spies have never seen any bundles carried into the house or out, though. It follows therefore that there needs must be a tunnel connecting the cellar with the sea. Therefore, it likewise follows that these rogues, with Sir George—who can never bide in England after this night—will run through the tunnel and take to ship. We will go across the beach and meet them as they emerge."

"Then in God's name, let us hasten!" begged the youth, wiping the cold sweat from his brow. "Once on that hellish craft, we can never get the girl again!"

"Your wound bleeds again," muttered Kane with a worried glance.

"No matter; on, for God's sake!"

CHAPTER 5
"INTO THE SUNRISE I GO"

Hollinster followed Kane who went boldly to the front door, opened it and sprang out. The fog had faded and the moon was clear, showing the black rocks of the beach two hundred yards away and beyond them the long evil-looking ship riding at anchor outside the foam line of the breakers. Of the guards outside the house there were none. Whether they took alarm at the noise inside the house and fled, whether they had received a command in some way, or whether they had had orders to return to the beach before this time, Kane and Jack never knew. But they saw no one. Along the beach the Rocks rose black and sinister like jagged dark houses, hiding whatever was going on in the sand at the water's edge.

The companions raced recklessly across the separating space. Kane showed no signs that he had just gone through a terrible gruelling grind of life and death. He seemed made of steel springs and an extra two hundred yard dash had no effect on nerve or wind.

But Hollinster reeled as he ran. He was weak from worry, excitement and loss of blood. Only his love for Mary and a grim determination kept him on his feet.

As they approached the Rocks, the sound of fierce voices instilled caution into their movements. Hollinster, almost in delirium, was for leaping across the Rocks and falling on whoever was on the other side, but Kane restrained him. Together they crept forward and lying flat on their bellies on a jutting ledge, they looked down.

The clear moonlight showed the watchers that the buccaneers on board the ship were preparing to weigh anchor.

Below them stood a small group of men. Already a long-boat full of rogues was pulling away to the ship, while another boatload waited impatiently, resting on their oars, while their leaders argued out a question on shore. Evidently the flight through the tunnel had been made with no loss of time. Had Sir George not halted to seize the girl, in which act luck was with him, all the rogues would have been aboard ship. The watchers could see the small cave, revealed by the rolling back of a large boulder, which was the mouth of the tunnel.

Sir George and Ben Allardine stood facing each other in hot debate. Mary, bound hand and foot, lay at their feet. At the sight Hollinster made to rise but Kane's iron grip held him quiescent for the time.

"I take the girl aboard!" rose Banway's angry voice.

"And I say no!" came Allardine's answering rasp. "No good'll come o' it! Look! There's Hardraker a-lyin' in his blood in yon cellar this minute account o' a girl! Women stirs up trouble and strife between men—bring that wench aboard and we'll have a dozen slit gullets afore sunrise! Cut her throat here, I says, and—"

He reached for the girl. Sir George struck aside his hand and drew his rapier, but Jack did not see that motion. Throwing aside Kane's restraining hand, Hollinster bounded erect and leaped recklessly from the ledge. At the sight the pirates in the boat raised a shout, and evidently thinking themselves to be attacked by a larger party, laid on their oars, leaving their mate and patron to shift for themselves.

Hollinster, striking feet first in the soft sand, went to his knees from the impact, but bounding up again, he charged the two men who stood gaping at him. Allardine went down with a cleft skull before he could lift his steel, and then Sir George parried Jack's second ferocious slash.

A cutlass is clumsy and not suitable for fencing or quick clever work. Jack had proved his superiority over Banway with the straight light blade, but he was unused to the heavy curved weapon and he was weakened and weary. Banway was fresh.

Still, for a few seconds Jack kept the nobleman on the defensive by the sheer fury of his onslaught—then in spite of his hate and determination, he began to weaken. Banway, with a cold smile on his dark face, touched him again and again, on cheek, breast and leg —not deep wounds, but stinging scratches which, bleeding, added to the general score of his weakness.

Sir George feinted swiftly, started his finishing lunge. His foot slipped in the shifty sand and he lost balance, slashed wildly, leaving himself wide open. Jack, seeing this dimly through blood-blinded eyes, threw all his waning strength into one last desperate effort. He sprang in and struck from the side, the keen edge crunching against Sir George's body half way between hip and arm pit. That blow should have cleft the ribs into the lung, but instead, the blade shattered like glass. Jack, dazed, reeled back, the useless hilt falling from his nerveless hand.

Sir George recovered himself and thrust with a wild cry of triumph. But even as the blade sang through the air, straight toward Jack's defenseless breast, a great shadow fell between. Banway's blade was brushed aside with incredible ease.

Hollinster, crawling away like a snake with a broken back, saw Solomon Kane looming like a black cloud over Sir George Banway, while the Puritan's long rapier, inexorable as doom, forced the nobleman to break ground, fencing desperately.

In the light of the moon which frosted the long quick blades with silver, Hollinster watched that fight as he leaned over the fainting girl and tried with weak and fumbling hands to loosen her bonds. He had heard of Kane's remarkable sword play. Now he had an opportunity to see for himself, and—born sword lover that he was—found himself wishing Kane faced a more worthy foe.

For though Sir George was an accomplished swordsman and had a name as a deadly duellist hereabouts, Kane merely toyed with him. With a great advantage in height, weight, strength and reach, Kane had still other advantages—those of skill and of speed. For all his size he was quicker than Banway. As to skill, the nobleman was a novice in comparison. Kane fought with an economy of motion and a lack of heat which robbed his play of some brilliance—he made no wide spectacular parries or long breath-taking lunges. But every motion he made was the right one; he was never at loss, never excited—a combination of ice and steel. In England and on the Continent, Hollinster had seen more flashy, more brilliant fencers than Kane, but he realized as he watched that he had never seen one who was as technically perfect, as crafty, as deadly, as the tall Puritan.

It seemed to him that Kane could have transfixed his adversary at the first pass, but such was not the Puritan's intention. He kept close in, his point ever threatening the other's face, and as he kept the young nobleman ever on the defensive, he talked in a calm passionless tone, never losing the play for a second, as if tongue and arm worked far apart.

"No, no, young sir, you need not leave your breast open. I saw Jack's blade shatter on your side and I will not risk my steel, strong and pliant as it is. Well, well, never take shame, sir; I have worn a steel mail under my shirt also, at times, though methinks 'twas scarce as strong as yours, to so turn a bullet at close range. However, the Lord in his infinite justice and mercy hath so made man that his vitals be not all locked up in his brisket. Would you were handier with the steel, Sir George; I take shame in slaying you— but—well, when a man sets foot on an adder he asks not its size."

These words were delivered in a serious and sincere manner, not in a sardonic fashion. Jack knew that Kane did not mean them as taunts. Sir George was white-faced; now his hue grew ashy under the moon. His arm ached with weariness and was heavy as lead; still this great devil in black pressed him as hard as ever, nullifying his most desperate efforts with super-human ease.

Suddenly Kane's brow clouded, as if he had an unpleasant task to do and would do it quickly.

"Enough!" he cried in his deep vibrant voice which chilled and thrilled his hearers. "This is an ill deed— let it be done quickly!"

What followed was too quick for the eye to follow. Hollinster never again doubted that Kane's sword play could be brilliant when he wished. Jack caught a flashing hint of a feint at the thigh—a sudden blinding flurry of bright steel—Sir George Banway lay dead at Solomon Kane's feet without twitching. A slight trickle of blood seeped from his left eye.

"Through the eyeball and into the brain," said Kane rather moodily, cleansing his point on which shone a single drop of blood. "He knew not what took him and died without pain. God grant all our deaths be as easy. But my heart is heavy within me, for he was little more than a youth, albeit an evil one, and was not my equal with the steel. Well, the Lord judge between him and me on the Judgment Day."

Mary whimpered in Jack's arms, coming out of her swoon. A strange glow was spreading over the land and Hollinster heard a peculiar crackling.

"Look! The house burns!"

Flames leaped from the black roof of the Banway manor house. The departing pirates had set a blaze and now it sprang into full fury, dimming the moon. The sea shimmered gorily in the scarlet glare and the pirate ship which was beating out to open sea, seemed to ride in a sea of blood. Her sails redly reflected the glow.

"She sails in an ocean of blood!" cried Kane, all the latent superstition and poetry roused in him. "She sails in gore and her sails are bright with blood! Death and destruction follow her and Hell cometh after! Red be her ruin and black her doom!"

Then with a sudden change in mood, the fanatic bent over Jack and the girl.

"I would bind and dress your wounds, lad," said he gently, "but methinks they are not serious, and I hear the rattle of many hoofs across the moors and your friends will soon be about you. Out of travail cometh strength and peace and happiness, and mayhap your paths will run straighter for this night of horror."

"But who are you?" cried the girl, clinging to him. "I know not how to thank you—"

"Thou hast thanked me enough, little one," said the strange man tenderly. "'Tis enough to see thee well and delivered out of persecution. May thou thrive and wed and bear strong sons and rosy daughters."

"But who are you? Whence come you? What seek you? Whither do you go?"

"I am a landless man," a strange intangible, almost mystic look flashed into his cold eyes. "I come out of the sunset and into the sunrise I go, wherever the Lord doth guide my feet. I seek—my soul's salvation, mayhap. I came, following the trail of vengeance. Now I must leave you. The dawn is not far away and I would not have it find me idle. It may be I shall see you no more. My work here is done; the long red trail is ended. The man of blood is dead. But there be other men of blood, and other trails of revenge and retribution. I work the will of God. While evil flourishes and wrongs grow rank, while men are persecuted and women wronged, while weak things, human or animal, are maltreated, there is no rest for me beneath the skies, nor peace at any board or bed. Farewell!"

"Stay!" cried out Jack, rising, tears springing suddenly into his eyes.

"Oh wait, sir!" called Mary, reaching out her white arms.

But the tall form had vanished in the darkness and no sound came back of his going.

ABOUT THE AUTHOR

ROBERT ERVIN HOWARD was born in the small town of Cross Plains, Texas, in 1906. His first story, "Spear and Fang," was published when he was eighteen, in *Weird Tales*. Over the next twelve years, Howard wrote over a million words of fantasy, Westerns, pirate yarns, detective and adventure stories for the pulp magazines. He is best known for his larger-than-life heroes: King Kull, Solomon Kane, Bran Mak Morn, and the greatest hero of them all, Conan, who swagger through exotic and far-off lands and times having fabulous adventures, conquering kingdoms and beautiful women with equal ease. Howard committed suicide on June 11, 1936, when he heard his mother had lapsed into a terminal coma.

THE WORLD OF ROBERT E. HOWARD

Born and bred in the rough, raw days just after the west was tamed, this country doctor's son lived out his short but amazing life in the small town of Cross Plains, Texas. Robert Ervin Howard, big and burly, was secretly a dreamer and a poet—a true pioneer in his own way.

A prolific writer of fiction, Howard struggled to gain recognition, writing for the pulp magazines that flourished in the 1920s and 30s. He ultimately became known as the leading American writer of heroic fantasy. His admirers included H. P. Lovecraft, Clark Ashton Smith and August Derleth.

Howard created his own world. A realm peopled with primitive men, barbarians, warriors, wizards, strong, beautiful women, and worshippers of dark gods in the forgotten lost civilizations. His heroes— CONAN, SOLOMON KANE and KULL—are all larger than life, believing in direct action, yet at the prey of emotional forces they can't control. Howard's stories are well known for strong plots, a colorful and vivid writing style, a marvelous sense of pace and action, and an emotional intensity that sweeps the reader along.

Howard's short life ended in suicide in 1936. However in 1951, a pile of unsold manuscripts was discovered. Arrangements were made with his heirs for their publication. Then much later, another batch of unpublished stories were found. Now, here are a number of those stories, many of them published in paperback for the first time.

For those who yearn for far-off and fanciful kingdoms of high adventure, of daring deeds and daring men who counter cunning with courage and conquer evil at any cost, read the stories of Robert E. Howard.

KULL

King of Valusia, he held the throne against plotting noblemen, priests of an overthrown serpent god and sorcerers who sought to topple this brawny barbarian. Combining mystery and splendor, wonder and horror, this book recounts Kull's adventures in the Forbidden Lake and among the eerily strange inhabitants of the Enchanted Land. (Available September)

SOLOMON KANE I: SKULLS IN THE STARS

The amazing exploits of the swashbuckling hero of the 16th century. Kane, who has the great courage to trust his instincts, is forever in pursuit of evil. This time the tumultuous trail takes him from England to a politically seething France, darkest Africa, and finally to the dangerous denizens of the Black Forest. (Available December)

SOLOMON KANE II: THE HILLS OF THE DEAD

Solomon's newest adventures in pursuit of evil lead him to the exotic jungles of the west coast of Africa. There, he encounters vampirism, meets an old sea-faring friend, finds the city of the unhumans, and ultimately discovers the survivors of an ancient civilization. (Available Feb. 1979)

(Look for all of these Robert Howard books, as well as the Conan adventures. Available from Bantam Books, wherever paperbacks are sold.)

OUT OF THIS WORLD!

That's the only way to describe Bantam's great series of science fiction classics. These space-age thrillers are filled with terror, fancy and adventure and written by America's most renowned writers of science fiction. Welcome to outer space and have a good trip!

☐	11392	**STAR TREK: THE NEW VOYAGES 2** by Culbreath & Marshak	$1.95
☐	11945	**THE MARTIAN CHRONICLES** by Ray Bradbury	$1.95
☐	02719	**STAR TREK: THE NEW VOYAGES** by Culbreath & Marshak	$1.75
☐	11502	**ALAS, BABYLON** by Pat Frank	$1.95
☐	12180	**A CANTICLE FOR LEIBOWITZ** by Walter Miller, Jr.	$1.95
☐	12673	**HELLSTROM'S HIVE** by Frank Herbert	$1.95
☐	12454	**DEMON SEED** by Dean R. Koontz	$1.95
☐	12044	**DRAGONSONG** by Anne McCaffrey	$1.95
☐	11599	**THE FARTHEST SHORE** by Ursula LeGuin	$1.95
☐	11600	**THE TOMBS OF ATUAN** by Ursula LeGuin	$1.95
☐	11609	**A WIZARD OF EARTHSEA** by Ursula LeGuin	$1.95
☐	12005	**20,000 LEAGUES UNDER THE SEA** by Jules Verne	$1.50
☐	11417	**STAR TREK XI** by James Blish	$1.50
☐	12655	**FANTASTIC VOYAGE** by Isaac Asimov	$1.95
☐	02517	**LOGAN'S RUN** by Nolan & Johnson	$1.75

Buy them at your local bookstore or use this handy coupon for ordering: